Perfectly Played
Initiation into Submission: High Protocol
By

KyAnn Waters

This is a work of fiction. Names, characters, places, and incidents are either the product of the author's imagination or are used fictitiously, and any resemblance to actual persons living or dead, business establishments, events, or locales, is entirely coincidental.

COPYRIGHT 2022 by KyAnn Waters
Cover Artist: LDM Graphics

All rights reserved. No part of this book may be used or reproduced in any manner whatsoever without written permission of the author except in the case of brief quotations embodied in critical articles or reviews.

Contact Information: kyannwaters@hotmail.com
Visit www.KyAnnWaters.com

Chapter One

Submission and danger are like a drug. And I'm an addict. I don't care who wields the whip. The pain and the fear are part of the high. If a Dom could play me perfectly, I'd be his.

"Tinker?"

The voice still sent shivers down her spine. The longing, once fierce and desolate, that ate at her soul wasn't for this man—not anymore.

"Yes, Sir." There was a time when she'd whispered his name, revealing the deep and twisted need that coiled within her. The need was still there, but not for the Boss. He wasn't hers…never was.

"Are you available? For play?"

Alex Ferraro hadn't touched her, hadn't calmed the maelstrom of fears and insecurities swirling within her in nearly a year. Not since Evelyn, the woman who'd claimed his heart. Once Alex had collared his submissive, a part of Tinker withered away. Another loss. Another heartbreak. One day there wouldn't be anything left to crush.

His eyes raked along her body, sending frissons of awareness over her flesh. Those dark eyes had haunted her nights for months—because of what they'd done to her, the pain, the discipline…the pleasure.

An ache pierced her heart with the need for the touch of a Dom who could alter her existence, shift the pull of gravity, and make her feel. That was what she waited for, the one she saved herself for. Submission in the dungeon would never be enough, only offering a moment of reprieve from the fierce needs inside of her.

Tinker needed a Master, to be owned. A complete possession.

"Yes, Sir." Her tongue felt thick in her mouth as she agreed to scene with him.

"I'd like to introduce you to my friend and associate, Luca Bruno."

The gentleman standing to the left of Alex stepped forward. His fingers gently grazed along her arm from elbow to palm, sending shivers over her flesh. He lifted her fingers and brushed a kiss to the back of her hand. "*Bellissima.*"

Tinker's gaze veered from Alex to the dark, whiskey-colored eyes of the man holding her hand. Not Alex, but another Dom. She lowered her gaze. This was her drug, what she needed. Who held the whip mattered less…until she found the one. "Sir."

"Luca is in town on business."

"My English is good," he said. "We should negotiate for our night."

Tinker's gaze made a slow slide to Alex. "Boss?" As Alex was known as in the Dungeon. The first time she'd come into his club, High Protocol had given her an escape from a life she no longer wanted to live. She still didn't. As a submissive, she bent her needs to serve her Master. Although he no longer touched her, in her mind, she still served the Boss.

"Luca," Alex said. "She may not be my submissive, but she is my responsibility." A tick worked along Alex's jaw. Then his gaze softened on Tinker. "She is magical, but she doesn't belong to you."

Warmth bloomed in her chest.

Alex kissed her forehead. "He knows the rules," he whispered. "In both English and Italian, he's been told no penetration."

She nodded. Maybe some people wouldn't understand why she'd protect her virginity. Not that she was inexperienced. Holding her virginity sacred meant keeping a part of her untouched for the Dom who would one day collar her, to want her forever.

Because Tinker held secrets, secrets too tempting to ever share. Not even with Alex.

Alex excused himself, making his way across the club and back to Ronan's observation platform. Ronan had recently become an owner of the club. She had occasionally done scenes with him. He had always put the dungeon above everything and everyone else, but she could count on him. She trusted him.

Because in her desperate need, Tinker didn't care if she drowned in the dark and rippling waters of BDSM. High Protocol had given her a way to survive. Ronan protected her, and the Professor had trained her.

Alex had ruined her. He'd given her a taste. Now, she spent every night in the dungeon, submitting to Doms, chasing the high she'd only touched with Alex.

Addiction was like that for some. Tinker couldn't be a casual user. And she couldn't stop. She didn't want to. Rather, she wanted to exist in the erotic haze that enveloped her when she was under a Dom's command.

The Professor wanted to save her. He'd shown her that submission had to be negotiated. Until trust was established, she needed to guard her needs and learn her limits.

If they only knew... Tinker only existed in the dungeon. Once she stepped outside the club, she trusted no one.

"*Innocente.*" The Italian man's gaze narrowed. "Innocent. I'm intrigued, Tinker."

The way he said her name, with that delicious accent, slipped through her veins like warm whiskey. She imagined not many women—or men—could resist his allure.

Luca rested his hand on the small of her back. The touch blazed through the thin, nearly translucent fabric of her slip dress. He towered over her, a well-honed body revealed in the expensive cut of his tailored suit. Luca oozed Italian wealth and charm.

But this was High Protocol—a BDSM playground for powerful men with decadent tastes. Tinker wanted to play. Arousal, anticipation, pain, and finally release. A salve to the cracks in her armor, her escape…her survival.

Luca escorted her to a seating area. Leather couches banked a couple of wide, thick cushioned chairs. He sat in the chair and indicated for her to sit at his feet.

Tinker breathed a sigh of relief. The unsettling intensity of his touch sent heated awareness into her breasts. She wasn't immune to his intoxicating influence.

Luca leaned back in the chair and plucked one if his dark, thick brows with his fingers. "*Innocente*," he said again. "Yet, here in this place."

The gold ring on his long, masculine finger boasted diamonds that winked from the lion's head. He wore another black and diamond ring on his left hand.

"You're married?" Rarely did she ask. But there was more than curiosity in his stare. She could feel his hunger.

Luca twisted the ring on his finger. "*Sì*, to my business. My family." The dark tone of his voice seeped into her.

The music from the club, the seductive lighting, and knowing he'd soon have her under his control spiraled into a heady mix of anticipation and trepidation.

Until recently, the Professor had exclusive control over her scenes. An unfortunate situation had left her unconscious and unsure of what had transpired with the Dom Apollo. She'd been scared, but she'd discovered her safeword gave her comfort. Even if she never found her limit, she used her word, like stretching an unused muscle, just to ensure the utterance would protect her.

Now that her probation had been lifted, she was free to negotiate her own terms. "Will you be in town long?"

He sighed. "No, I must return to my home in Italy. I'll be returning often until my business with Alex is concluded. Should we discuss our play?" He rested a hand on her head, smoothing her hair. "*Bellissima.*"

"*Sì,*" she said, using his language, and lowered her gaze.

"This pleases me, Tinker." His voice, an exotic sound from his lips, flowed hot through her. "Look at me."

She lifted her gaze to his. Dark stubble shadowed his angular jaw. Hypnotic eyes fringed with dark lashes sparked with barely banked desire. He inhaled, flaring the nostrils of his straight yet defined Italian nose. Wide, lush lips curved into a wolfish smile. Nearly black hair, in a gentleman's cut, kissed the shell of his ears.

He raked his fingers through the soft waves on top.

"Hard impact?"

"Yes."

He leaned forward. "Hard limits?"

"No penetration."

"No sex?" he asked. "You're sure?"

She smiled. "No sex."

"Can I kiss you?" He grazed his finger along her cheek, sliding his thumb over her upper lip.

"Yes."

Luca kissed her, a feathering of lips, a whispered promise of seduction. Her tummy tumbled. She rested her hand on his thigh. Hardened muscles tensed beneath her palm. His fingers curved around the nape of her neck, urging her closer. When she leaned in for another kiss, his tongue barely touched her upper lip, just as quickly slipping away. She pressed her lips together, savoring the tease of pleasure.

"Alex has gifted me his private room this evening. Will you join me there now?" He held his hand out to her as he stood.

Tinker curled her fingers around his, her chest tightening with anticipation.

Although she could show him the way, she remained a step behind him as he led her through the dungeon. She cast a glance over her shoulder to the observation platform. Alex watched her, his gaze intent, but his arm was possessively wrapped around Evelyn. A smile found his lips, and then he turned away.

Unlike the pain of punishment, rejection cut deep. Alex had left her scarred. With negotiated scenes, she wouldn't endure the anguish of emotional bleeding.

Luca slid his temporary membership card through the lock to the private rooms. His polished Italian leather shoes echoed off the marble hall.

They stopped in front of the door. Tinker's heart raced. She swallowed. Her throat thickened with fear. Not because of Luca, but because, at one time, she'd believed herself in love with Alex, and he'd brought her to his room. She didn't want to color her night with Luca with the memory of another.

The door opened. Luca stepped to the side for her to enter. A light in the corner cast a golden glow over the elegantly decorated room. The steel bondage bed, riggings, frames, and crosses at odds with the leather, opulent decadence, and luxury.

The door clicked shut.

"In the dungeon, you will not wear clothing."

She nodded.

"Strip." One word, spoken low and controlled, sent an icy tingle along her spine.

Comfortable in her nudity, Tinker slipped the wide straps from her shoulders. The thin material pooled at her feet. Already braless, she tucked her thumbs under the elastic of her plain, white, bikini-cut panties and pushed them down her legs. Gathering them, she folded her panties along with the dress, leaving them on the floor, and setting her sandals on top. She stood with her arms at her side and her head bowed.

"Your safeword, Tinker?" His large hand splayed across her belly as he positioned behind her. Lips brushed against her shoulders and slipped across her skin to the tender tendon of her neck. He gently bit, sucking her flesh.

Shallow breaths tightened her chest. "Pickle, Sir."

"No penetration," he confirmed, his breath hot against her ear. "Here are *my* rules."

The cool air of the room puckered her nipples, but the dangerous edge to his voice sent chills over her.

"*Per favore*—ah, excuse me. No, English is best for you. Please will be the only word from your lips. Do you understand?"

"Please," she whispered. Her body trembled with his nearness. The scent of his cologne clung to him. She ached to bury her nose in his neck, taste the hotness of his flesh, and feel the power of his tightly controlled form against her.

The teasing glint in Luca's eyes morphed into an erotic yet brutal glare. Did he see her as a challenge? He would know soon enough how pliant and submissive her nature was.

"You will not come from our play."

She refused to lift her gaze. "Please?" How did she convey that she would need her release? The pleasure of BDSM was too ingrained within her to be quieted. But without his permission, she doubted her body would crest.

"Ah, sweet Tinker, if you want to come, you'll give me the pleasure of your body."

Her gaze lifted to his. Knots tightened her guts. The temptation, the whispered words, the powerful aphrodisiac of a Dominant in control tightened and coiled ready to strike.

Her heart pounded in her chest. She stared into his eyes, eyes flashing with the delicious arrogance of a Dominant. Luca Bruno clearly was a man used to getting what he desired.

But he couldn't demand the one thing she held sacred. "Pickle."

His gaze narrowed as a half-smile twisted his lips. "*Mi scusi*. Excuse me."

"I'm sorry we couldn't negotiate a scene." She picked up her dress. Not bothering with her panties, she slipped on the sandals and draped the dress over her head as she went to the door.

Luca caught her and wrapped an arm around her waist. His touch released a riot of butterflies in her belly. She froze, fear and desire warring for dominance in her thoughts. Luca had the aura of a man not to be toyed with, but also the lure of a man who could master her mind and body.

"I am disappointed." He released her. "Have a good evening, *amore*."

Tinker slipped out the door. As she strode down the hall, her emotions overwhelmed her. She'd only just met him. She shouldn't care, yet he'd left her with a hollow ache inside. She pushed through the door into the club, searching for the one face she needed.

Her gaze lifted to the platform. Alex laughed with Evelyn, Ronan, and Ronan's submissive, Claire. Those weren't the arms she needed around her.

In the distance, light glinted off a bald head. She weaved through the crowd. Sensing her approach, his gaze shifted to hers.

"Hey, Tink, what's wrong?" The Professor opened his arms, and she stepped into his embrace. Thick tattooed biceps circled her shoulders. Resting her cheek on his solid, warm chest, she soaked in the calming energy of her best friend.

"I used my safeword."

He chuckled and his eyes brightened. "Good girl."

She stared up into his face. "Yeah, but we hadn't started our scene yet."

His brows furrowed.

She didn't want to tell him the whole story. She just wanted to move on from an unfortunate misunderstanding. Maybe it was the language barrier. Although the no sex stipulation seemed to be clearly communicated. "The Boss has a business associate in town, an Italian. He specifically asked if I'd do a scene with him. Do you think Alex will be upset with me?"

The Professor nodded toward a man storming across the room. "You can ask him."

Alex approached. His sharp gaze rested on her. Lips pulled into a hard line. "Tinker, what happened?"

She shook her head. "Nothing."

The Professor's hold on her tightened. "You have to tell him, Tink." His attention shifted to Alex. "I don't know, Boss, but she said she used her safeword."

"We have different needs," she explained, "so I decided not to scene with Luca. Is that going to cause an issue for you?"

"Of course not," Alex said. "Did Luca cross a line with you?"

"He understood my rule," Tinker said. "No sex. But he had rules, too. He didn't like mine, and I didn't agree with his."

The Professor lifted her chin. "What were his rules?"

She licked her lips. "He wasn't going to let me come."

Alex bristled, and the Professor laughed.

"What a dick," the Professor said.

His large hand trekked along the ladder of her spine. She'd been at the end of his flogger many times. Trusted him to take away her senses, strip her fears, and take her into subspace. She'd felt his calloused fingers on every part of her body, felt the sting of his whip, and the tender touch of his aftercare. But the Professor wasn't emotionally connected to her or anyone else that she was aware of.

Alex cupped her cheek. "I apologize. I'll speak to him."

She rested her hand on his arm. "You don't need to. He was a gentleman in every other way. He's going back to Italy soon so why add to the situation. I'm fine." She rested her palm on the Professor's chest. "I'm going to ask this Dom who knows what I need for a lesson, and then I'm going home for the night. I'm good."

Alex nodded. He inhaled as if he planned to speak, but something over her shoulder grabbed his gaze. "Excuse me."

He stepped away, approaching Luca as he entered the dungeon.

Luca's focus drilled into her. Arrogance radiated from him, confident in his dominance. There was something about him. A mysterious edge appealed to her submissive nature. That made him dangerous.

The Professor rested a hand on her hip. "Tinker?"

"Thank you."

His rough knuckles brushed her cheek. "For what?"

"For making me strong enough to say no." Controlling men were her weakness, her drug of choice.

"What do you want, beautiful?"

"A demonstration." She wanted Luca to see what he'd lost in negotiations.

"Are you sure you're my sweet, innocent submissive?"

No, she hadn't been innocent in a long time.

***

Luca feigned indifference. Alex stood in front of him, hands casually stored in his front pockets. But the glint in his eyes chased a sliver of fear along Luca's spine. Not that he felt physically threatened by the Dom of High Protocol, but he needed Alex's business connections in the States.

"What the fuck, Luca?" Alex growled as his gaze narrowed.

"A misunderstanding." He slid his hand into his suit pocket, running his fingers over the soft cotton of her panties. When he'd taken her into the private den, he'd anticipated another willing club sub. Instead, she'd defiantly countered his demand with her safeword.

"We go back a long time. I made it clear she was under my protection."

Luca followed him to the observation platform. "I agreed to her negotiations." He chuckled. "If I wasn't going to come, neither was she."

At least, not until he had his hands and mouth on her. He wanted more from her than a pain slut's orgasm.

"You're a dick. You'll never get another opportunity."

Perhaps not. Or perhaps their negotiations had just begun.

"Pets are like the pound," Luca said. "There is always another prettier pussy to pet." He swallowed the lie. Yes, pretty pussies, but none that understood their power the way Tinker understood hers, holding onto the treasure only offered once.

Lights in the dungeon dimmed and spotlights illuminated the demonstration area. Luca turned to the blonde, petite woman standing nude in the middle of the stage.

Alex leaned over. "Tinker intends to show you what you're missing out on."

Everyone could see what he'd missed. Delicate but shamelessly alluring. Ripe, dusky pink nipples centered on small, pert breasts. Her arms hung limply at her sides with her hands resting on her trim thighs. Her milky, smooth flesh glowed beneath the lights over the platform. Only a hint of hair covered her pussy. A pussy she claimed had never been pleasured.

The burly bald Dom that had been holding Tinker stepped onto the stage. He covered her mouth with his. Luca's gut tightened, and his balls warmed. "She belongs to him, no?"

Alex leaned against the railing. "No. She belongs to the dungeon."

"Who is this man?"

"He's called the Professor. He specializes in training submissives. Tinker had a scare, needed to set boundaries." Alex smiled. "You, my friend, experienced just how good the Professor has been at teaching her about hard limits."

Luca kept his gaze locked on Tinker. The Dominant carefully braided her hair. Then he faced her. Tinker licked her lips and stretched her mouth. The Professor inserted a two-inch ball gag into her mouth and buckled the strap around her head. Two alligator clamps dangled from the gag around her face. The Professor sucked her beautiful tit into his mouth, only for a moment to tighten her nipple. Then he pinched the clamp onto the tip.

Luca stared at her. Tinker's response to the Dom heated his jealousy to a fevered pitch.

She moaned, and her eyes slid closed.

The Professor guided her to a steel frame in the center of the room and whispered in her ear.

Tinker lowered her gaze, reached into the Dom's pants, and stroked his cock.

"Untouched." He glared at Alex. "*Innocente*?"

Alex laughed. "I never said she was innocent. I said she was a virgin."

Luca snapped his gaze to the woman with lust-filled eyes and a sinful body.

Her legs spread, and the Dom dropped to his knees, securing her ankles to the frame with neoprene cuffs. He remained on his knees, running his hands over her calves, touching the back of her knees as he kissed her pelvis. In a slow, sensual path, he slid his tongue over her flesh, abstaining from tasting the one place Luca wouldn't resist, the sweetness of a woman's desire.

The Dom's hands skimmed her hips as he rose and then those hands curved around to her ass. The Professor smiled, and Tinker gripped the sides of the frame.

Luca strained to hear the Professor's words as he spoke.

"Removing your hands from the frame is your signal to stop the scene."

She nodded.

While gently tugging on the alligator clamps, the Professor landed a stinging slap to her ass. The angle of the frame allowed some viewers to see the pleasure/pain on her face while others watched her firm, luscious ass absorb the continued swats of his hand. The slaps warmed her flesh, painting a rosy blush to her skin.

Tinker whimpered, arched her back, and braced against the impact.

The Professor praised her, promising more.

"Can you handle the thick cane?"

Spit glistened at the corner of her gagged mouth. She nodded once.

The Professor cupped her crotch.

A flare of anger rushed through Luca. This man touched her.

Tinker shuddered. A lump welled in Luca's throat. The man slid his finger along her clit and gathered her nectar, but he didn't penetrate her.

A virgin…and a beautiful, sexual beast.

"Not yet," the Professor said. "I decide when you come."

He gripped a thick rattan cane with a woven handle. With quick flicks of his wrist, he tapped the cane against her blushed buttocks. Tinker shivered, her eyes closed, and her knuckles whitened as she gripped the steel frame.

Someone in the crowd gasped as the Professor landed the first sharp hit.

Tinker moaned, and her nostrils flared as she tensed against the pain. Another crack of the cane welted against her flesh, this time to her upper thigh. Her lips thinned as she struggled for breath.

"Breathe, Tink." The Professor's voice seemed to soothe her as her body relaxed, but then he raised his arm, and brought the cane down across the buttocks again.

Tears slipped from her eyes. Saliva dripped from her chin.

"Good girl," the Professor praised. "Come for me, Tinker." He tapped his fingers against Tinker's pussy. She cried out through the ball gag, her legs trembling and her body convulsing.

Luca stepped closer to the edge of the observation platform. He needed more, to see her every reaction, to hear her breathless panting, to smell her arousal. She swayed, her body becoming pliant. Rather than allowing her to settle into the euphoric high of subspace, the Professor landed another series of strikes. She cried out with each punishing blow.

Cream trickled down her legs. One orgasm rolled into the next as the Professor shifted between wielding the cane and sliding his thick finger along her clit. Her hips rolled, thrusting against his palm.

A soft whimper fell from her lips as one hand released the steel frame. The Professor dropped the cane. He released an alligator clamp from her nipple and sucked hard on her tit. Her thin fingers clutched his bald head, anchoring him to her breast.

The Professor unbuckled the ball gag. She barely had time to wipe the spit from her chin before his lips were on hers. He kissed her, plundering her mouth.

Held captivated, Luca adjusted his cock in his pants. *Bellissima.*

Once the Professor had her free from the frame, he carried her to a small aftercare area at the edge of the stage. Her Dom stroked her legs, massaged her buttocks, and ran his hands over her body.

Alex rested a palm on Luca's shoulder. "Now you can see why we call her Tinker. She sparkles."

Luca stiffened, the touch intruding on the moment playing out in his mind. She should have been his tonight, but another Dom tended to the strikes, smearing cream on the bright bloom of color and the raised red welts.

Luca clenched his jaw. He wanted to know more about her.

In business and in life, he took what he wanted. If negotiations were required, he learned his opponent, discovered their weakness, and then exploited it to his advantage. In his dealings with Alex over the years, they had developed a mutual respect, both hungry for victory whatever the cost.

Both hungry for position and power.

Luca considered them friends. However, Alex served a purpose. Legitimate dealings in the US sheltered his less palatable endeavors. He wasn't opposed to skirting the boundaries of ethics to get what he wanted. He'd cut the head off his competition, never settling. Even if by devious measures, he'd take what he wanted. Now, that was Tinker. According to Alex, she belonged to the dungeon. Not for long.

"Excuse me," he said to Alex. "I must make my apologies."

Luca stepped from the observation platform. Anticipation slipped through his veins. The Professor had been brutal in his strikes.

Tinker had descended into subspace, her body responding to the pain and control. He'd never seen such a powerful submission.

The lights in the demonstration area dimmed. Members returned to their socializing. Luca weaved around the perimeter of the room. Like the hawk with his precision gaze on his prey, Luca approached the Dominant—and the submissive who would be his.

The bald man laughed, his forearm resting along Tinker's thighs as she sat in his lap. Once again, the thin dress draped her svelte form. She sipped a bottle of water. Another woman sat near them, her body cloaked in leather. Lips, bright red and smiling, devoured Luca as he approached.

"Excuse me." His gaze rested on Tinker. "I wanted to let you both know how much I enjoyed your demonstration."

Tinker's spine stiffened.

The Dominant roamed his hand over her thigh. "Not as much as I did."

The woman with the bright red lipstick laughed.

"Trinity." Tinker bit into her lip.

"Ah, yes, I'm told many Dominants enjoy her charms." Property of the dungeon, her submission open for the taking. Luca was used to taking what he wanted.

Her gaze snapped to his. "Are you here to renegotiate?"

A slow smile tilted his lips. "No, *bellissima*."

There would be no more negotiations. He would have her. All of her.

Tinker's palm rolled over the bald Dominant's head. "I'll see you tomorrow."

"You're leaving?" His grip tightened on her hips.

"Yes." Her gaze shifted to Luca. "Safe travels back to Italy."

She stood. The shadow of her nipples teased the sheer fabric of her dress. The Professor rose, and her thin arms roped around his shoulders. He kissed her temple.

Luca met the Professor's glare, then he turned to follow Tinker.

"Leave her alone." The calm words floated across the distance between them.

Luca smiled as he walked away. No, he wouldn't be leaving her alone.

"Tinker?" He caught up with her in the foyer. "Allow me to walk you to your vehicle."

"That isn't necessary." She continued her way outside the club.

Fuck, she would make him follow like a puppy. "Stop."

As if unable to resist, she paused and pivoted toward him. A flash of indecision crossed her features. "Why?" She tilted her head. "I can guess. You're probably not used to one of your submissives telling you no."

He touched her cheek, and her breath caught. "Not just submissives." The rest of the statement hung unspoken between them. No one dared deny him. "I would like to take you to dinner."

"Even if you weren't going back to Italy, I'm not interested in sharing a meal with you. I'm not going to scene with you, and I'm not going to—" She licked her lip. "—I'm not going to fuck you," she said with a lowered voice.

"Not interested in dating, not interested in fucking, but you spend your evenings in a BDSM dungeon, coming on the fingers of whomever holds the cane."

Her head tilted. "Or whip or flogger or strap."

"That is only the discipline of BDSM." Luca wrapped his fingers over her ribs. "What of the Master who would command your obedience? Perhaps you need more than pain."

She swallowed.

"I'm not negotiating for you." He leaned in, sliding his palm to her back, holding her closer. He molded her small frame to his chest and brushed the edge of her ear with his lips. "I will be the one with the whip, *amore mio*." He touched the fluttering pulse in her neck with the tip of his tongue. "But I want something in return."

"We've already had our negotiations." Her palm rested on his chest. With gentle pressure, she put space between them.

"Ah, sweet Tinker."

"You don't know if I'm sweet."

Curling his fingers around the nape of her neck, he jerked her petite frame against his solid chest and covered her mouth with his. With her gasp, he slid his tongue into her mouth. The palm on his chest tightened into a fist as she leaned into the kiss, sliding her tongue into his mouth.

Luca growled, twisting her braid in his fist, and pulled.

Tinker cried out. He bit her lip, then fiercely claimed her mouth again, sucking her tongue, and crushing her body to his. She whimpered, becoming pliant in his arms. Her hips rocked into his, feeling the heat and hardness of his erection.

Luca broke the kiss. "You're right," he said, staring into her eyes as the lust simmered between them. "Not sweet. You're sin and innocence. And you will be mine."

Chapter Two

Tinker drove through the streets in her little yellow compact. She turned left onto a dead-end street and weaved through the trees, her headlights approaching the twelve-foot-high security fence. The gate swung open. An armed security guard nodded as she drove passed. Along the quarter-mile cobblestone driveway, she veered under two archways.

Outdoor lighting illuminated the front of the sprawling thirty-thousand square-foot mansion on a twenty-five-acre estate just north of the city. She parked in front of the house. By morning, the car's interior and exterior would be detailed and the gas tank topped off.

She'd lived at the Thomas Estate her entire life, not that it ever really felt like home. Leaving her sandals next to the door, she passed through the open foyer. Sterile, immaculate, exactly as it had been as long as she'd been alive. Paintings hung on the walls. Pictures once graced the shiny surface of the grand piano.

Not anymore.

In fact, there weren't any family photos in the house with the exception of the huge oil painting above the fireplace in the main room. However, since she rarely entered that room, she wouldn't be reminded of what she'd lost.

"You're home."

She paused at the hard voice from the shadow of the room. "Yes, and I don't want to argue."

Keith Hudson, her bodyguard, stepped away from the wall.

"How am I supposed to protect you if I'm not with you?" His jaw clenched, and his massive arms crossed in front of his chest.

Tinker started up the stairs to her suite of rooms. "I don't need protection at Protocol."

He grunted. "Knowing you're in that place, what they do to you, it fucking kills me."

"I'm not asking for your permission."

He snorted. "Right, not from the man who would give his life for you. Just the men who would break you."

She paused, her gaze resting on his. "They can't break me, Hudson. I'm already broken."

"Mia—"

She ignored him and continued up the stairs.

In her bedroom, she shrugged out of her dress and strode naked into the bathroom. With a touch of a button, a waterfall of warm water cascaded from a stainless-steel plate suspended from the high ceiling. Soft amber lighting filled the space.

She stepped into the water, tipping her face to the gentle spray and washed remnants of Tinker away for the night. Here, she was Mia

Evangeline Thomas, heiress to the billion-dollar Thomas diamond empire.

Water stung the abrasions to her buttocks and thighs.

"Mia?"

"Yes, Poppy?" Both Poppy and Hudson had been with her since before the end of the Thomas dynasty.

"Will you need the cream tonight?"

Mia ran her fingers over the tender flesh of her buttocks. "Not tonight."

"Okay, you know to come get me if you need me."

Mia smiled. "Thank you. Get some sleep."

"You, too."

Alone with her thoughts, she combed her fingers through her braid, let the warm water sluice over her tender nipples, and simmered with the memory of Luca's lips on hers.

And you will be mine. His words weighed heavy on her. She ached to belong to one man, her Master. To live as Tinker, leaving Mia in the past where she belonged, dead and buried with the rest of her family.

Mia stepped from the shower and folded herself into a thick, plush towel. She dried her body and squeezed the water from her long hair.

Poppy had removed her dirty clothes. A sheer nightgown draped over the turned-down bed.

Tonight, she didn't want the luxury of her bed. She needed the comfort of her submission. Crossing the room, she opened the double doors leading to her dungeon—a room never seen by a Dom.

Inside the darkened room, she drew in a calming breath. The scent of leather surrounded her. She dropped to her hands and knees and crawled across the floor to a slave pallet at the foot of the bed. She curled into a ball, covered her nude body with a thin blanket, and closed her eyes.

Images of Luca filled her mind. With a moan, she remembered the soft curve of his determined lips. His gaze had raked her body, tightening her nipples, and making her wet. In the cool air of her dungeon, she recalled the warmth of his breath on her flesh. She rested her palm on her neck, ghosting her fingers over the place he'd kissed her, a reminder of how his lips had felt.

But he wanted a scene, wanted her body, and he would leave her when he returned to Italy. He'd take everything and then, even as a billionaire heiress, she'd truly have nothing precious left to give.

***

The next morning, she'd felt as if she'd barely slept. From both the bruising intensity of the caning and the hard night on the pallet, her body was deliciously tender. Shuffling sounded from the bedroom. "Poppy?"

"Yes, Miss?"

Mia stood. "Just coffee this morning."

"Of course. Will you be having it in the office with Mr. Sutton?"

"Is that this morning?" She had a meeting with the head of her financial advisory team, Grant Sutton. Nothing changed, not in her worlds. Decimal points moved on the bottom ledgers of her business empire. In the dungeon, the name and face of her Dominant changed. Neither world bled into the other.

In the dungeon, she was Tinker. And although her staff understood she lived what they would consider a secret, dangerous life after dark, only Poppy and Hudson knew where she went. No one knew with whom she shared her submission.

Hudson hated what she did. Sometimes she wondered why he didn't just leave her. But he stayed by her side, trying to protect her, even while she pushed him away. Only Poppy understood. Because not all Doms had taken care with her after a scene, Poppy occasionally took care of her. Hudson would want revenge.

She shivered remembering the night Apollo had wrapped his fingers around her neck. The breath play had come after an intense period of sensory deprivation. She hadn't realized anything was wrong until it was too late.

Now, she had to be more careful. Trying to reach new depths in subspace, hoping she could replace one pain with another wasn't working.

Tears burned her eyes. She still lived in her nightmare. The Thomas Empire hung like an albatross around her neck.

"Tell Grant I'll be with him shortly."

Poppy nodded and quietly left the room.

Mia fingered the gray, flared pants and cream-colored blouse Poppy had laid out for her today. A bra and panties matched the clothes, as well as casual gray mules with a one-inch heel.

After she dressed, she fingered her hair into a stylish messy bun, added a touch of makeup and a squirt of perfume, then she headed to the west wing of the house to continue liquidating more of the monster that had destroyed her life and everyone she'd ever loved.

Grant stood when she entered the office. He pushed his glasses onto his nose, and his thin lips curved into a smile.

"Would you mind if we had our meeting on the terrace?" she asked. She didn't want reminded of Oliver, not today. The office had been his sanctuary until…

She blinked and squared her shoulders. She hated this, hated everything to do with the Thomas legacy. Hated the insecurity making her heart pound. Sweat dampened her armpits. Ollie suffered under the weight of the massive responsibility. She refused. She didn't want to make decisions, didn't want the burden. Money couldn't save her.

***

Later that night, she once again stole into the night. She parked her small compact car in the lot across from High Protocol. Leaving Mia behind, she entered the club as Tinker.

Joel, bouncer, and security for the club, smiled. "How's my girl?"

"Good." She smoothed her hands over her short leather miniskirt. A leather chest harness, laced in the front, covered her breasts but left her midriff exposed. Black leather, calf-high boots encased her legs. As usual, she wore her hair in a tight braid down the center of her back. "Is Alex here tonight?"

She really wanted to inquire about Luca, but the last thing she needed was for Joel to casually mention her interest. Better he thought she wanted time with the Boss.

"Haven't seen him, but he could have come through the private entrance."

"Thanks, I'll look around." Tinker entered the dungeon. The familiar scents of leather and sex permeated the air. Music pumped through the sound system. High Protocol wasn't just a dungeon. This was where she felt comfortable in her own skin. Anonymity cloaked her insecurity.

"Tinker." Trinity waved from the seating area to the left.

Tinker approached and gave Trinity a kiss on her cheek.

Trinity was a Domme with a sadist streak, leaning toward torture. Her hooded submissive sat at her feet, a choke collar around his neck and a steel cage confining his cock.

Tinker sat next to Trinity. Until this week Tinker hadn't seen her around in a while. "I'm glad you're back."

"We were short staffed at the hospital." Trinity worked as a hospital administrator. They'd played in paired scenes over the years, but never together. Trinity wasn't into sex, neither giving nor receiving. She had a gift for humiliation and degradation. High-powered executives loved relinquishing their power to the tiny woman. A simple word, spoken in her commanding tone, had them shivering, afraid of displeasing their mistress.

Tinker envied them—with the exception of sex. Tinker held her virginity, but she needed to please as much as she needed permission to come. As she spoke with Trinity, she continued to search the crowd.

Search for the whiskey-colored eyes that darkened with dangerous longing.

She pressed her fingertips to her lips. The kiss had been hot, controlling, and arrogant, but it was the words that tempted her. A Master who would command her obedience, give her more than pain. Did he mean those words?

Ronan strode through the dungeon. She tracked his movements. A quiet night at the dungeon meant no demonstrations. No one socialized on the observation platform.

"I need to find the Professor," she said to Trinity.

Trinity laughed. "Tell him to be good to you."

"I don't have to. They're all good to me." Except the one who'd scared her with his rules. Now, he was in her head, twisting her thoughts into a reckless whirlwind of indecision. She needed him tonight, needed Luca to demand her submission.

Tinker wandered toward the rear of the club. She clamped her lower lip between her teeth as she scoured the room. He wasn't here. Disappointment welled within her.

She moved to one of the aftercare couches and curled into the corner. The whir of a whip sounded in the distance. A submissive cried out. Tinker closed her eyes, her body instinctually responding to the aural stimulation.

Voices filtered through the music, the Italian accent impossible to miss. She sat straighter and glanced over her shoulder. For a moment, absorbed in their conversation, they didn't notice her. She averted her gaze. Her heart raced, and her breaths came in shallow bursts. He was here. Would he remember his words from last night?

She knew the moment Luca noticed her. His conversation stopped, and she could feel the weight of his stare.

A shadow fell against the couch. Shivers chased along her flesh. She lifted her gaze to his. "Sir."

Those dark eyes focused, seeing into her, knowing the effect he had on her. A simmering awareness unfurled within her, spreading through her like a warm elixir. Tonight, he wore form-fitting, black denim, and an open V-neck loose-fitting Henley. Dark hair dusted his chest.

He held his hand out to her, not an invitation or request, but a silent command. A pounding roared through her mind, drowning out the music, chattering voices, and drone of the club. Awareness narrowed to Luca, the primal glint in his eye, and the obedience he expected. She slipped her fingers into his.

"Tinker?" Alex questioned.

Luca ignored Alex, cupped her cheek, and brushed his lips against hers.

Tinker sighed, the heat of his lips melting against hers. She tasted the seam of his lips, and then opened her mouth in invitation to take more.

Luca growled. "Leave us," he demanded of Alex.

Alex waited with his gaze locked on her. Tinker waited for Luca to give her permission to speak. After a moment, Luca nodded.

"We've renegotiated," she said.

Alex reached out to touch her, but Luca stepped in front of her. "No one touches her now that she's mine."

The words, vehemently spoken, stirred her emotions. *His*. But only for a scene.

Alex smiled. "Maybe you do understand our Tinker. Then if I don't see you again this evening, I'll meet you in the office tomorrow. We can finish up our business."

"Tinker—" Alex seemed poised to say something to her, but then his gaze softened. He shifted his focus to Luca. "She's yours for tonight but don't forget, She belongs to me and the dungeon. You leave tomorrow. If you leave her in pieces—"

"I won't take from her anything she doesn't freely give."

"My private den is available."

Luca kept her hand in his as they once again made their way through the dungeon. As soon as they stepped into the corridor through the private doors, he pressed her against the wall. "Did you think of me last night?"

"Yes."

As his lips roamed over her neck, his fingertips sought the smooth flesh of her midriff. Quivers rippled over her belly, a shuddering anticipation.

"Did you lie in bed and touch yourself?" He bit the lobe of her ear, then sucked it into his mouth. "Or had the Professor's fingers given you all you needed?"

"No."

"No?" He crushed his lips against hers, plundering her mouth in punishing intensity.

Tinker whimpered. She kept her hands at her sides, afraid to touch him.

Finally, he ripped his lips from hers. "I fucked my fist, thinking of you."

She sucked in a breath. "I didn't touch myself."

Luca's grip on her waist tightened. "The Professor gives you all you need?"

She gasped as his fingertips dug into her hips. The lion ring cut into her flesh. "No."

"Tinker, you'll hide nothing from me."

Her gaze searched his. Only Tinker could be honest and share with him her needs and insecurities. "No Dom has given me everything I need. I don't masturbate in my bed. Why would I?" Her mouth suddenly dry, she swallowed. "I can't come without permission."

"Tonight, we shall see if I can please you." His heated gaze seeped into her. "And if you can please me."

***

Luca opened the door to Alex's private den. Like last night, a single lamp illuminated the room. Tinker, in a sheer gossamer dress had fooled him into believing her innocence. This submissive, dressed in leather, reeking of sex, revealed the truth.

She was both heaven and hell. Luca wasn't looking for a halo. In his world, he was destined to burn.

Luca stalked the perimeter of the room. "Unless you are ordering lunch, I will not hear you say pickle. You're safeword is *rossa*."

Tinker nodded.

"Were you gagged because you're unable to remain quiet when instructed?" He gripped the front of her corset, ripped the thin laces loose, and exposed her breasts.

Tinker startled, her chest rising and falling with sharp breaths.

"So beautiful." His aggression softened to a delicate pinch to her budded nipple.

He stepped back and stripped off his shirt. Her gaze followed the lines of his chest, trekking lower across his abdominals. His cock kicked against the tightness of his jeans. The zipper growled in the quiet room as he lowered it. The elastic band of his boxers kept his dick pressed against his groin, the head dripping pre-cum, and his balls grew heavy and warm.

Luca took her hand in his. "Touch me, Tinker."

He rested her palm on his sternum. Her fingers, long and delicate, floated across his skin, tightening his gut.

Tonight, he'd give her a taste, enough to whet her appetite. He would gain Tinker's trust. Too many had already used her for their need for control. He was no different. But he would be the last.

He slid his lips over hers. "I want to see your beautiful body."

She stepped back. With a shrug of her shoulders, the corset, with the laces shredded, tumbled to the floor.

Keeping her gaze on his, she slipped the buttons at the side of her skirt and shimmied the leather mini over her hips. Then tucking her thumbs into the elastic of her panties, she stripped them down her thighs. After she stepped out of them, she lowered the zippers on her boots and tugged off one and then the other.

"Turn around," he said.

Tinker lowered her head and faced away from him. Luca's hands curled into fists. He had been an arrogant fool. From the first innocent touch, his heart had pounded within his chest. A master of manipulation, he'd toyed with her. And lost.

But she must have felt the same pull because standing before him now, she was marred with the reminders of another man's pleasure. Jealousy churned in his gut. Dark bruising shadowed her upper thighs and buttocks. He gripped her ass, digging his fingers into the marks left from the caning.

She whimpered.

"You won't know where his begin and mine end." He seduced her, weaving his intensions with a submissive's needs. "The marks on your body will all be mine."

He sucked her neck, ensuring he branded every part of her.

Her hands curled into fists, her nails cutting into her palm. She leaned into him.

Luca inhaled her perfumed scent. Heat slipped through his veins. She was petite, seemed almost timid. Yet, she radiated with unleashed sexual energy. Submissive, yes, but like him, she had a lion's heart. He'd glimpsed her strength when she'd walked away from him. Once again in his lair, he wanted her to roar.

He released her. "On the bench, *bella*."

Tinker crossed to the paddling bench. Bracing her knees on the lower pads, she crawled over the table. Her forearms rested on the bench, hiking her ass in the air. Her smooth, soft skin trembled beneath his fingertips. That he made her nervous heightened his anticipation. Need fired through him.

He secured her calves to the bench with leather bands. Then he dropped to a squat in front of her.

"The rules are the same," he said and brushed a kiss to each of her hands. He then banded more straps over her arms, locking her to the bench. He smiled knowing his words would be misinterpreted but needing her to know he would control their scene and their pleasure. "You will not come from our play."

She sucked in a breath. "Please," she whispered, fear clouding her piercing eyes.

"Ah, Tinker. You will have your release, but not from the impact of my strap." He kissed her lips. "Trust me, *bella*. I intend to have you, as Alex said, in pieces." He crashed his lips onto hers, spearing his tongue into her mouth.

Hesitant at first, she then sighed, surrendering to his kiss. Her tongue touched his and entered his mouth.

Luca groaned. "*Sei mio*, Tinker. You are mine."

He selected a two-inch wide and eighteen-inch-long Scottish tawse. The leather split into twin straps. He ran his palm over the curve of her ass.

"You will remember our first night together," he whispered and landed the first strike. Tonight, he'd ruin her for any other.

She tensed, her body stiffening with the stinging intensity.

He bent and laved his tongue over the quickly rising welt. "You are sweet…in the right places."

The next several strikes were light and teasing. A bloom of crimson brightened her thighs and buttocks.

"Please," she whispered, her head falling forward. "More."

The sound of her voice cut through the fog of lust swirling in his mind. He stripped out of his jeans. He circled the bench, stood in front of her, and fisted his cock. "Open your mouth."

Tinker's gaze lifted to his.

He brushed his fingers over the droplets of sweat at her hairline. Her breath gusted across her lips, but a pleading need for more reflected in her eyes. He fisted her braid. "Suck."

She swallowed hard, then opened her mouth and wrapped her lips around the head of his cock.

Luca groaned, pushing deep into her mouth. "When you beg for more, it will be for my cock."

She moaned, her tongue swirling around the head. Fuck, she was breathtaking. Her cheeks hollowed as she sucked him harder, her teeth grazing the length of his shaft. Too intense. Being inside her mouth felt too good. His balls drew up close to his body.

"Enough." He pulled from her lips. Crouching before her, he wiped a smear of saliva from her chin with his thumb. "We both wait to come."

She nodded.

Maneuvering around the table, he positioned to continue his teasing slaps. The tawse snapped against her, biting into the flesh of her thighs. Last night during the demonstration, the Professor had delivered most of his strikes to her buttocks. The bruising was dark and brutal.

Emotions rolled through him, driving him to brand her as his. He brushed a kiss to her buttocks, opening his mouth, and laving her tender flesh with his tongue. Her mewls of pleasure permeated the air.

With her thighs spread, cream glistened on her pussy. Gathering her wetness on his finger, he painted her rosette.

Tinker moaned, instinctively backing into him. He chuckled. His sweet virgin tempted his fingers to play. But she'd made her rules. No penetration. Luca spread her cheeks and licked her from clit to rosette.

She cried out. Trembling started in her legs and quickly overtook her body. He couldn't deny her, couldn't deny himself. Just one against his tongue.

"Plea—" She stopped before completely forming the word.

Hating the rules, because her word denied him the taste of her cum, Luca slapped her with the strap, then moved in front of her. No words were needed. Her mouth opened, and she greedily swallowed his cock. He fisted her braid again and fucked her mouth. This time he didn't pull out. He pumped his hips, thrusting past her teeth, gliding across her tongue, and bumping the back of her throat.

Tears dampened her lashes, rimming her eyes as she sucked, her throat massaging the head of his dick with every swallow.

Heat streaked along his spine. His balls tightened, and he erupted. Shards of pleasure ripped through him. Muscles in his arms flexed, his abdominals clenched, and a roar burst from his lungs. Hot jets of cum bathed her mouth. She swallowed and sucked. His cock stretched her lips, and her nostrils flared as she fought for breath.

As the last tugs of pleasure rippled through his cock, Tinker's mouth slackened, and his dick slipped from her lips. She trembled, her body a tight wire of pressurized need. She moaned, her gaze on his. "Please," she whimpered. "Please. Please. Please." The words were barely a whisper.

Luca tore the restraints from her arms and legs.

She shivered, clawing at his back as he carried her to the bed. Her mouth hungrily devoured his neck, biting and sucking.

"Now you can come." Luca settled her on the bed, spread her thighs wide and latched onto her clit. He sucked hard, bit into her tender, soaked flesh, and unleashed a storm of aggressive convulsions.

She screamed. Fluids gushed from her core. Her release only made him more ravenous. Licking, biting, sucking. Her head thrashed, and her fingers clutched the bedding. "Sir." Her back arched as another climax had her in the throes of ecstasy.

Luca softened his touch, gently tasting her folds. Her sweet cream floated over his tongue. Inhaling deeply, he drew in the scent of her sex. As her breathing slowed, her thighs dropped open. He kissed her navel and nuzzled against her ribs as he crawled over her body.

"*Bellissima*," he whispered then sucked her breast into his mouth.

Tinker gripped his shoulders, clinging to him like a lifeline. Braced on outstretched arms, he settled his hips in the cradle of her thighs. She stiffened beneath him.

"Trust me, *bella*." Hard again, he rocked his hips, sliding his shaft along her folds. "I need to feel you on my cock."

"Sir?" Her hips rolled. "I don't want to say the word."

"I promise. For both of us." He kissed her lips, grinding his dick against her mound. "Trust me. Wrap your legs around me."

Tears slipped from her eyes. He kissed her harder, rocking his hips, crushing his cock against her wet pussy.

Tinker's thighs locked against him. She arched, pressing her breasts to his chest. The change in her breathing, the flutter in her chest, and the slickness between her legs revealed her building need.

"Come for me, Tinker. Come from my cock." He slid against her clit.

A guttural moan tore from within her. Her teeth sank into her lip as she came.

"Luca," she wailed as her nails scored his back.

Luca hissed. Heat streaked along his spine, his mind numbed, and his body jerked. Hot ribbons of cum jetted from his dick, spurting onto her stomach. Muscles in his arms tensed as he braced his weight and rode the dizzying waves. As the violent tremors ebbed, he lowered onto her, letting her absorb the weight of his body.

Their mingled scent of sex surrounded him. He kissed along her jaw, whispered words in Italian. She was magical. Her soft touch roamed over his back, along his lats, and onto his buttocks.

He rolled to his side and pulled her close. "I need to take care of you but don't want to let you go." Curling her into his chest, he kissed the top of her head.

Long moments passed. Their breathing returned to normal. The quiet of the room surrounded him. Contentment was an elusive emotion, yet now, with her, the stress and noise of his life mellowed to a distant hum. She rested a hand on his sternum, her fingertips tickling the hair on his chest.

"You were perfect." He touched her, praised her, however something was wrong between them. Could she be angry from yesterday? He tilted her chin. "Tinker, about yesterday. Accept my apology." It hadn't been the language barrier, but his arrogance. "I shouldn't have toyed with you. I didn't respect your limits. I promise, I respect the rules we both have. I won't betray your trust."

"Thank you. Is our scene over?" Her innocent eyes stared into his.

He combed a stray tendril of her silken hair from her cheek. "Were you not satisfied with our play?"

"I am, Sir." She traced the muscular edge of his pectoral. "But I feel fine now. Do you want me to leave?"

Hovering over her, he opened his mouth over her collarbone. "Why would I want you to leave?"

"Because—" She hesitated, shifting her gaze away from him.

Luca lifted his head. "Tell me."

She seemed to weigh her response. "Because once aftercare is done, the scene is over. I go back to the Professor, and the Dom finds someone or something else to do. I'm not cuddled. Not kissed like this."

"Where is the pleasure in only discipline?" He closed his mouth over her nipple. With a taste, his cock stirred. A ravenous desire to power over her rushed through him. No, he was nowhere near quenching his hunger.

She arched into him. "Discipline is the only pleasure I need."

He bracketed her ribs, gripping her tightly. "Ah, Tinker. You need so much more." He bit into the flesh of her breast.

Tinker sucked in a sharp inhale and grasped his head, curling her fingers into his hair. He sucked hard, bringing blood, a bruising hickey, to the surface. The sweet taste of her sealed her fate. Determined to make her his, he anchored her to the bed, and staked claim to her body. Worshipping her with hands and mouth, he brought her to the edge of delirium.

"Do you want to come?" he asked.

"Please."

The simple word threatened to fray the thin hold he had on his voracious desires, to unleash the darkness always lurking beneath the surface "Our scene is over, but your words still have consequences."

Tinker licked her lips. "Please," she said again, curling her fingers around the base of his shaft and stroking the length.

"*Cazzo*!" Fuck. His fingers wrapped around her neck, pinning her to the bed. He slid his other hand between her thighs and grazed her clit. Her juices soaked his fingers. "So wet. Come on my fingers, Tinker. Show me how hungry your pussy is for my touch."

Her hips bucked. His grip on her neck tightened, but not enough to choke or restrict her breathing. Only enough to show her his control, to show her that she could trust him to hold her immobile and rip orgasms from her with more than the pain of his strap. With a tortured groan, she came. Too many orgasms had left her overly stimulated and raw.

He felt the same. Shudders vibrated through her as her eyes closed and her body attempted to bow off the bed, only the pressure of his hands held her.

With her fingers still curled around his dick, she pumped her fist, milking him, driving him to release. Her grip tightened. He released his hold on her neck as he erupted, his orgasm passing the threshold of pain.

Tinker continued to pump her fist. She shifted her position and closed her mouth over the head, sucking hard.

Luca roared. The head of his cock was too sensitized for the pleasure of her mouth. Yet he endured. Who had the power in their exchange? When she'd spoken the word *please*, she condemned herself to licking his cock clean…and sentenced him to an agonizing climax.

He tunneled his fingers into her hair, loosening her braid. "I'm going to lock you away and keep you for myself."

She smiled as she sat back on her haunches. A whimper pursed her lips. She shifted onto her hip.

He slid from the bed and crossed to the wall of cabinets, shelves, and drawers. He gathered cream, ice, a towel, and a bottle of water from the small fridge.

"Over my lap," he said and repositioned on the bed with his supplies.

Tinker's beautiful ass, bruised and blooming with color, draped over his thighs. She pillowed her cheek on her clasped hands. He gathered the medicated aloe cream on his fingers then gently coated her flesh.

"When do you go back to Italy?" she asked.

He sighed. "I'd planned on returning tomorrow." He bent forward and kissed her shoulder. "After an evening with you, I find I'm not as eager to leave." Not that he could spare more than one more day. "I have obligations at home. Sadly, my time isn't always my own."

She shivered as he ran a piece of ice over the brightest welts. "I understand."

Did she? One night wasn't going to be enough to slack his need for her. If anything, her responses had only piqued more interest. "My business with Alex is going to take months to complete. I'd like to extend our arrangement."

Tinker carefully sat and twisted to face him. "I'd like that."

He cupped her cheek. "I'll be gone about a week."

Maybe ten days.

Long enough to appease Giada. If he spent too much time from home, she went from demanding bitch to uncontrollable cunt. He'd be done with her if it weren't for his son, Savio. "Wait for me."

Tinker nodded.

***

With his and Alex's current business concluded, Luca had returned to his suite at the hotel, ordered dinner, and packed his bags. The plane was ready, but he couldn't bring himself to leave. A beautiful, blonde nymph occupied his thoughts. Even if he wanted to, he couldn't contact her. Without a name, he couldn't find her number.

No doubt, she would be at Protocol. If she was there…he would be as well.

Luca checked his watch. With the time difference and the flight time, he needed to leave tonight by one. They would fly all night to get him back to Italy.

Picking up his cell, he called Carlo, his consigliere, speaking to him in Italian. He loosened his tie. "Hold the plane. Something has come up, and I'll be delayed."

Carlo always traveled with him. More than security for Luca, the six foot, two-hundred pounds of Italian muscle would take a bullet for him—and fire one. Carlo never questioned his orders. Always had Luca's back. And never wavered in his loyalty.

An hour later, Luca had his bags in the back of the sedan. Bullet-proof, blacked-out glass, luxurious, and Carlo behind the wheel.

"No need to wait," he said to Carlo as the vehicle pulled up to the entrance of High Protocol. "Just be back in time to get me to the plane by one."

"I'll wait here in case your plans change. Does she know you'll be late?"

By *she* Carlo meant Giada. "My personal time is no longer her concern."

Carlo laughed with a snort. He met Luca's gaze in the rearview mirror and jutted his chin toward the door of the club. "She must be beautiful."

Luca's response was an arch to his brow. "No later than one."

Carlo nodded.

Luca stepped out of the car and buttoned his jacket as he crossed the street. He ran his access card through the lock, entered the club, and nodded to the security guard. With the confidence of a man on a mission to claim what belonged to him, he strode through the door to the dungeon.

His fingers clenched and unclenched as his gaze skated over the club, searching for her. The one who took his focus, had his gut tight, and his dick hard. He moved through the crowd, making his way toward the observation platform.

The one they called Ronan nodded in his direction. "The Boss isn't here tonight."

"I'm not here on business," he said. "I should be on my way back home, but I wanted to see Tinker once more before I left."

Ronan lifted his gaze. "I saw her with the Professor an hour ago. They're usually in the back. I'll walk with you."

The bitter taste of jealousy filled his mouth. She wasn't expecting him. "Is Alex's room available?"

Ronan smiled. "No problem, but it's up to Tinker."

A commotion erupted in the corner. Tinker's head fell back as she laughed. Luca approached. The group quieted.

"Ronan." The Professor acknowledged the club manager, but his gaze locked on Luca, and his lips turned down in a contemptuous sneer. "Thought you were heading back to Italy."

"Later tonight. There are benefits to owning a private jet."

Ronan sat next to the Domme in leather. "Good to see you back, Trinity. Are you ready to sink your teeth into some unsuspecting toy?"

She snapped her teeth. "I break all my toys."

Ronan laughed.

Although he didn't want to socialize, Luca sat in an empty chair. His gaze rested on Tinker. Her chest rose and fell with rapid breaths. He waited, waited for her to meet his stare. The Professor wrapped his arm around her shoulders.

Luca tilted his head, staring into the Dom's eyes. He clenched his jaw and forced a slow smile.

Jealousy had sunk her teeth into the Professor as well.

Tinker stiffened as she lifted her head. Her gaze met Luca's. Without uttering a word, she stood from the couch. A long, silk skirt hung low on her hips. A loose, flowing top exposed one shoulder, cut across her collarbone, billowing around her torso. Without a bra, the sheer fabric revealed her dusky nipples.

She wore his marks. Bruises marred the porcelain skin of her belly. Several hickeys tinted her neck. Beneath the skirt, he could imagine the colors, like an erotic painting on flawless flesh.

"Tinker?" the Professor questioned, reaching for her hand. "We talked about this." His eyes seemed to plead with her. "Safe, sane, and consensual."

"I promise, it was." She pulled her fingers from his.

"Are you good?" Ronan asked her.

"Does she look good?" the Professor spit. "She's got choke marks on her neck. I'm not dealing with another fucking Apollo."

With his eyes, Luca directed her to a spot on the floor next to his feet. She dropped to her knees next to him.

Luca collared her neck, aligning his fingers with the bruises he'd left, and tipped her face to his. "Put their worries to rest, *bella*." He sipped her lips. "Tell him." Another kiss. "I'm impatient to have you alone."

Her eyes grew heavy with lust. She licked her lips. "I'm good."

Luca stood, taking her hand in his. "Enjoy your evening," he said to everyone. He allowed his gaze to harden on the Professor because he wanted no misunderstanding. Tinker was no longer in need of his protection.

Once in the corridor to the private den, he tugged her closer. "I had to see you again."

Her gaze locked with his, and her brows furrowed.

"That surprises you?" He stopped in front of the door to Alex's private room.

"Not that you want to see me," she said, entering the room. "But that you would change your plans to stay."

"I've only delayed my departure." Giving him one more chance to leave an impression and to emphasize his intentions toward her.

Tinker's gaze tracked his movements as he strode to the bar filled with private stock. Alex wasn't a drinker, yet he stocked only top shelf. Shrugging out of his jacket, Luca considered the selection. Something to calm his nerves and temper his needs because anticipation welled in his gut.

After last night, he wanted another taste of her pussy, to feel her come against his tongue. The scent of her perfume followed him, tempting him to force her acquiescence.

Luca poured two inches of cognac into a tumbler. He didn't want her obedient from fear or submission. Not only did he want her desperate and begging. He wanted devotion.

"You're drinking?" she asked.

Luca tipped the glass to his lips and sipped. He sat in a deep leather chair and stretched his legs out in front of him. "Take off your clothes. While in a dungeon with me, you will be nude."

His gaze remained focused on her, waiting for her to do as he asked.

Indecision flitted across her face. Her gaze shifted from his eyes to the drink. Her teeth grazed her lower lip. And then she lifted her blouse over her head.

Under his stare, her nipples puckered. He remembered well the sweet taste of her breasts. Tucking her thumbs into her skirt, she pushed the silk fabric, along with her panties over her hips.

Luca tipped the glass for another sip.

"Kneel."

Without hesitation, she lowered to the ground.

"Come to me, Tinker. On your hands and knees."

Tinker crawled across the floor, her back arched like a kitten.

"I'm torn, my pet." He leaned forward to cup her cheek. "I needed you to be here tonight, but I find you in the arms of the Professor. Should I praise you…or punish you?"

She swallowed.

"Don't worry, I don't expect an answer." He leaned back in the chair. "Fuck." He tossed back the rest of the cognac and slammed the glass to the table. He fisted her hair, tightening his hold and bringing her mouth to his.

Tinker's soft gasp spurred him into wanting more. Grazing his tongue over her lips, he speared into her open mouth. He growled and tugged her onto his lap. He covered her breast with his hand, squeezing, molding her into his palm.

She whimpered. "Please."

Pleasure ripped along his spine. "There are no rules tonight, *amore mio*. No discipline. Just pleasure." He closed his mouth over her nipple. He gently sucked, pillowing the turgid tip against his tongue. "Sweet."

Feathering kisses in the valley between her breasts, he teased and tasted his way to her other nipple.

"The pleasure will hurt so good." He bit hard, raking his teeth over her nipple.

Tinker cried out, her nails clawing his neck as she gripped his head, holding him tight to her breast. Luca released her nipple and stood with her in his arms and carried her to the bed.

As she moved into the center of the mattress, he tugged his tie loose and slipped the silk from around his neck.

"Spread your legs."

Her eyes locked with his as her thighs slowly opened.

He unbuttoned his shirt, slipped the buttons on the cuffs, and shrugged out of his sleeves.

"Touch your clit."

Her delicate fingers slid between her folds, gently rubbing a tight circle on the swollen bud.

Luca crawled onto the bed next to her.

"What are you doing to me?" Her fingers stilled.

"Worshipping you the way you deserve." He covered her fingers with his. "Don't stop. I want you to come."

With his hand over hers, she slid deeper into her dewy softness. He rained open-mouth kisses along her ribs, sipped across her belly, and sucked the flesh below her navel. He marked her with hard, demanding kisses. With his other hand, he set the tempo with her fingers beneath his.

The aroma of her arousal sifted through his senses. Whimpers and mewling need slipped from her lips, and her breathy panting filled the room. Pressure built in his balls. She made him crazy with desire. Her body responded, her need for pleasure eclipsing his need for release.

He recognized in her the same restlessness within him. She needed more than this, more than demanded orgasms, and more than servicing her Dom. Just as he wanted more than a shared pet in a BDSM dungeon.

"Feel what you do to me," he whispered in her ear.

She hesitantly cradled his groin, running her fingers over the hard ridge of his erection.

He chuckled. "No, here." He lifted her hand to his racing heart. "You're like a caged tiger, needing to be tamed, but fighting against the desire to unleash. Is it anger?" His—hers—fingers strumming against her faster, vibrating over her clit. "Hatred?" More pressure, tightening the circle of stimulation. "Is this enough, to come on command, to soothe the beast inside you?"

Tinker jerked hard, her body convulsing as she wildly stroked her clit. "Luca," she gasped.

He kissed her, claiming her mouth with tongue and lips. Her cream slicked their joined fingers. Small eruptions rippled through her core as her hips rolled and her pussy quivered. He leveraged higher, squeezing her cunt as the last fluttering ripples faded.

Bringing their joined hands to his lips, he then tasted her cream, running his tongue over her fingers, savoring her essence.

Her eyes widened. "What do you want, Luca? My submission? My virginity?" Her hand cupped his cheek. "You live in Italy, and I'm here."

"You excite me, Tinker. An arrangement with me won't be easy." Luca kissed her fingertips. "I've been called ruthless and cruel." He skimmed his fingers over her flesh, puckering her nipples and causing her to shiver. "I can give you the discipline you crave." He stared hard into her eyes. "Because when you're ready, you'll be mine."

Chapter Three

Tinker couldn't do this, couldn't stare into Luca's dark, hooded eyes as he kissed her fingertips. He was too intense, wanted in too deep. Quivers rippled through her as his palm rested on her belly. He made her wet and needy, but he also sent shivers of fear through her. Her lips whispered please, but she couldn't admit, not even to herself, that she pleaded for more of his emotional torment.

Last night had shattered her thoughts. Men—Doms—used her for their needs, the control, the dominance, the pleasure of pain. But she wasn't disciplined to strip her emotions bare, to surrender and find the freedom of subspace. She used them to dilute the pain of life with the pain of punishment.

Until Luca.

Not even Alex had promised passion, but every sip of Luca's lips had her craving more. She wanted to touch him the way he touched her, to freely roam her hands over the hills and contours of his chest, to trail her fingers over the fine, feathering hair bisecting his defined and ribbed abdominals. She wanted him naked, stretched out next to her so she could curl her fingers around his thick, hot length.

But he hadn't given her permission. Already she feared his rejection.

He checked his watch, sighed, and sat. A storm darkened his eyes as he traced the marks on her neck with his thumb.

"So beautiful." His gaze lifted to hers. "I've delayed longer than I should have." His tongue flicked against her jaw. "Although I have to go, you are a temptation I have no desire to resist."

Heat pooled in her belly, sinking lower and making her wetter.

"Come with me." He cradled her breast. Leaning over her, he closed his mouth over her nipple.

She sighed and arched into his deliciously wicked mouth. His teeth grazed the edge of her areola. A flash of fear zinged along her spine, waiting for the pain of his bite. "Where?"

He chuckled, the sound reverberating into her skin. "Home with me." He raised his head.

A flare of uneasiness tripped her heart. She leaned up on her elbows. "To Italy?" Her brows furrowed. Then she smiled. "I wish, but you know I can't." She touched his cheek. "I'll see you when you come back."

Luca clasped her wrist in his iron grip, rolling her to her back and pinning her to the mattress. "Nothing is impossible. Say yes." He kissed her neck. "Only for a few days, then we'll be back. You're safe with me, *bella*. If you trust

Alex, you know he would never put you in the arms of an enemy."

His mouth muddied her thoughts. A few days with nothing but to exist under his wickedly erotic dominance. She could leave her life and just be his Tinker.

Reality crashed into her thoughts bringing a wave of panic. She fought the building anxiety threatening to make her run. The question…Was she running to him or away from him? She desperately wanted to say yes, to escape for a few days.

"I can't," she whispered. Tinker couldn't travel, and Mia would never exist in a world with Luca. "I don't have my passport."

"You don't need one. We're taking my jet to a private landing strip."

"My clothes? I can't leave for a few days with only a skirt and top."

"I'll buy you whatever you need." With a gentle persuasive touch, he reached between her legs.

Tension coiled low in her in belly.

"We'll relax by the pool and sip wine after dinner." Searching out her clit, he slid a finger into her wet folds.

Shivers raced over her flesh, pressure building, the need to come sliding closer.

"I'll eat your pussy and make you come as the sun sets." A slow circle with his thumb played her clit. "I know what you need, Tinker. I'll discipline you in my dungeon."

She moaned, rushing toward the crest.

"I love seeing my marks on your flesh. You have my word. I won't take what isn't mine."

She rolled her hips, grinding into his touch.

"Say yes, Tinker, and come on my fingers."

"Yes." A hard contraction ripped through her body. "Yes," she cried again, gripping his arm as her body bucked.

Luca kissed her, meshing his mouth to hers, tangling their tongues. He tasted of cognac and danger. She would be without the security of the dungeon, without her identity, and at the total discretion of a man she didn't know.

***

This was crazy. She'd be at his mercy. Tinker's heart thundered. Words of warning filtered through her thoughts. Ronan had called her reckless. The Professor's firm but gentle reminders on how to protect herself went unheeded. There was no safeword for how she was feeling. Nothing could have prepared her for the emotional assault of this man.

Luca's hand rested on her lower back as he approached a black sedan outside the club. A huge, muscular Italian stepped from the driver's seat.

"I've got her," Luca said, opening the rear passenger door. "Tinker, this is Carlo."

Carlo smiled and returned to the driver's side. "Any stops on our way?"

"No. Sorry I'm late." Luca checked his watch again.

Carlo laughed and pulled away from the curb.

In the back of the darkened car, Luca ran his palm over her flank and his nose along her neck. "You're trembling."

Not from the chilled night air. "I know."

His strong fingers squeezed her thigh. She ached to touch him. Fear kept her hands at her sides.

"Do I make you nervous?"

"Yes," she breathed. "Can I touch you?"

"In private, always."

Scooting closer, she sought the heat of his body.

"Perhaps we should negotiate our expectations," he said.

Yes, because she didn't have boyfriends. Actually, she didn't have anyone outside of High Protocol. Just Poppy and Hudson.

"Wait," she stammered, glancing over her shoulder. They'd already left the city behind, now heading to the airport. She didn't have her phone, her wallet, or ID. In the club, Chris the bartender kept her things stowed behind the bar. Ronan and the Professor were right to be concerned. "I don't have my phone. I should let—I need to let Alex know I've left."

"Carlo."

The driver handed Luca a phone over the seat.

"I'll text Alex." His thumbs cruised over the keypad.

"What are you telling him?" She had no idea how Alex would respond. Not that there were any miscommunications on their relationship. Tinker belonged to the club, to the scene. She was their demo dolly, willing to submit until she found the Dom who would want more than a scene, more than her submission.

Her eyes searched Luca's. They had a connection. His touch, his kiss, the strength of his voice, and the finality of his words all collided in an irresistible intoxication.

"That you're with me." A slow smile curled his lips. "Would you like me to tell him you no longer belong to Protocol? That you're mine now."

"No, you'll make him worry." She banked her emotions from both the fear and the exhilaration of his words.

"I don't want you to worry either." He handed her the phone. "Let your family know you're with me and available at my number." He brushed a tendril of hair from her cheek. "Anyone who needs to know. Family, your employer. I want you to feel safe with me."

Tinker only knew two numbers by heart. A text wouldn't be enough. And she couldn't call Hudson. He'd come after her. She called Poppy.

"Hello." Her hesitant voice warmed Tinker. "It's me."

"Mia, what's wrong?" Panic laced Poppy's words. "Are you hurt? Should I get Hudson?" She always worried. She didn't understand Tinker. Or why she'd turn her back on everything that should have been important to Mia.

"Nothing's wrong, and no, I'm not hurt." Not wanting to be overheard, knowing she would be, she still tried to put distance between her and Luca. She lowered her voice. "Absolutely do not say anything. Make an excuse."

"What kind of excuse?"

"Whatever will work. I'm with a friend so there is nothing to worry about." Her fingers instinctively covered her neck and the bruising of her flesh. "I won't be home for a few days. Save this number. I don't have my phone with me."

Poppy lowered her voice. "Are you in trouble, Mia?"

She smiled. No more than usual. "Can you make arrangements to get my car from the lot?" Poppy and Hudson were the only ones who knew where she went at night. Because Poppy had seen too much, she'd become scared for Tinker. "I'm fine, but I won't be available for a couple of days. Can you make an excuse to Grant?" She was supposed to meet with him again this week, downtown with the entire team. "I need to go."

"I don't like this, Mia. Hudson is going to be livid."

"I'll handle it when I get home. Don't worry."

"I always worry. Be safe." She paused, obviously hearing the hitch in Tinker's voice. "Don't let the men hurt you."

Tinker ignored a flicker of guilt.

"I have to go." She disconnected the call and handed the phone back to Luca.

"Who is Grant?" He slipped the phone into the inside pocket of his suit coat.

"Someone I know from my work."

"Good." Did she hear a note of jealousy in the clipped word?

"We're here." Carlo parked the car in the stall next to the private hanger. He exited the vehicle, slid his palm inside his jacket as he scanned the area, and then opened the rear door.

Luca stepped from the car and held his hand out to Tinker. Bitter wind whipped her hair, painfully puckered her nipples, and billowed her skirt. She folded her arms across her chest.

He shrugged out of his jacket and draped it over her shoulders.

"Thank you." She slipped her arms into the sleeves, soaking in the warmth of his body and the scent of his cologne.

Carlo grabbed the bags out of the trunk, and Luca escorted her to the stairs leading to the main cabin of the jet.

A woman waited just inside the plane. "*Signor*, Bruno," she greeted him.

He spoke a few words in Italian. She nodded her head, turned away, and began preparing food.

Stainless steel appliances and a state-of-the-art galley comprised the forward portion of the jet. A leather couch and chairs positioned in front of a large theater-style, flat screen television.

"Are you hungry? I've ordered a light meal for us."

"Thank you." Tinker clasped her hands in front of her.

Carlo lumbered into the cabin, shrugged out of his jacket, and pulled his gun from the harness strapped across his massive torso. He flopped onto the couch, flipped on the television, and stretched his legs.

Tinker's gaze locked on the gun. All her life she'd been surrounded by armed guards. Her pulse took a bit of a jolt. Luca had wealth. Most of the members at Protocol were wealthy, but few had armed escorts.

He held her hand as he led her past Carlo. "It's late for him. He's used to a nine o'clock bedtime."

Carlo flipped him off. "Someone needs to watch your back. Late night clubbing," he grumbled. "Kinky motherfucker." His gaze shifted away from Tinker, and the rest of what he said was in Italian.

"Ignore him," he whispered against her ear. His hand rested on her hip as he walked backward toward the rear cabin of the plane, bringing her with him. "Ignore everyone."

Tinker's head tilted as his mouth slid along her neck.

The plane engines roared as they entered the bedroom suite. The pilot spoke in Italian over the intercom.

Luca maneuvered her onto the bed.

"Luca?" Her hands rested on his chest as he hovered over her, forcing her to the mattress.

Italian came over the intercom again. "Prepare for takeoff," Luca translated for her as he stretched out next to her. "Thank you for saying yes." Crinkles creased the corners of his sparking eyes as he smiled. "I want you with me." His fingers brushed the edge of her face. "We hardly know each other, but I suppose that is the beauty of a BDSM club. I'm not interested in sharing you with the dungeon."

"You won't have to, not this week."

He growled and banded an arm over her as the plane raced down the runway, then swooped into the air.

"Okay," he said, sitting up. "I can't introduce you to my family as Tinker."

She jolted upright. "Your family?"

"*Sì.*"

The woman from the main cabin entered the room with his drink. He stood and spoke to her in Italian.

"Our dinner will be ready in twenty minutes." He sipped the amber alcohol.

"Luca, I can't meet your family. I thought—" She wasn't sure what she thought. Her need for his touch had made the disastrous decision to get on his plane without her purse, phone, or ID. "I thought you were returning for business." Not to introduce the submissive he'd played with twice to his family.

Meeting families wasn't something she did because she didn't socialize outside of Protocol. She slid from the bed and paced across the floor. "Oh my god, this was a mistake."

Luca leaned against the wall. His gaze narrowed on her.

Think. A burning fear roiled in her belly. "Maybe I could just stay at a hotel."

Maybe she could get Poppy to figure this out. Because she had so few people in her inner circle, it also meant she had few people to call on for help.

Hudson would go ballistic knowing she was out of the country without identification, money, or security. As a former Navy Seal, he idled at intense. He'd seen too much of the world. And Alex wasn't an option. Actually, she couldn't trust anyone through the club.

"Are you done?"

Her gaze snapped to Luca. "What?"

"Whatever *this is* going through your head? It's my son's birthday. Savio is five today. I made him a promise to be there."

"You brought me to a *birthday party*?"

He pushed away from the wall. "*Sì*. Tinker—" He sighed, extended his hand, and introduced himself. "Luca Roberto Bruno. Roberto after my father. Same for my brothers. We all have Roberto as our middle name. I'm twenty-seven, and I have a five-year-old son." When she didn't shake his hand, he wrapped his arms around her waist. "What else? I wanted to marry my first love when I was eighteen, but we never did."

"Why?"

He released her and took a step back. "Our families didn't approve. Life would have been…difficult. Marriages in my world are for family alliances."

"Love isn't enough?"

"No. If you ask my father, he will tell you love makes a man weak. When I think of the life Camilla would have had as my wife, I'm glad she is now married to a car salesman with a bunch of babies." He smiled. "She is happier, too. I work in my family's business. I need nothing more than a beautiful woman on my arm in public, and a submissive on her knees in the bedroom. And you are the most beautiful woman I've ever seen." His gaze connected with hers. "And I have yet to learn your name."

"Mia Tho— Toliver." She said the first word that popped in to her mind. She couldn't say Thomas. An international man of wealth and privilege might recognize the name. "I'm twenty-four." She smiled. "Virgin, so no kids and never been married. Never been engaged."

He sat on the end of the bed and sipped his drink. "Do you want marriage and children?"

She shrugged. "I expect to be collared. Marriage—" No, she wouldn't get married. Money made powerful men dangerous. Her gaze shifted to Luca. He was dangerous enough. "I don't need to be married. And honestly, I don't know if I'll ever have kids." She smiled and lightened the mood. "Unlikely since I'm still a virgin."

"I have three brothers and a sister. Marco is the oldest, Stefano and Orlando come next." He finished his drink. "Then there is Anna."

"And they will all be at the party?"

"Yes." His lips lifted into a smile. "You will like my sister. She is always looking for a new partner in crime for her mischievous activities, however, you'll be next to me."

"I don't have anything to wear." She couldn't go to a little boy's birthday with her nipples showing.

He pointed to the far side of the room. "Look in the closet. I'm sure there is something appropriate for a birthday party."

Tinker crossed to the wardrobe. Inside, there were designer handbags, lingerie, and a small amount of jewelry in the top drawers. Beautiful clothes draped from hangers in the cedar closet. Why did he have a closet full of women's clothes? All in her size and designer brands. "Are these Anna's?"

He laughed. "Take whatever you want."

Their meal arrived as she fingered through the clothes. She pulled out a form-fitting, high-necked, sleeveless black dress. If she wore a jacket or shawl, she'd be able to hide her bruises.

Luca reclined on the bed, nibbling on fruit and cheese. "Are you hungry, Mia?"

She froze at the way her name floated across his lips. Darkly erotic and full of promise.

"Take off your clothes."

Tinker—Mia, couldn't resist the magnetic pull of his voice. She slipped off her skirt and pulled her shirt over her head. She gathered her clothes, neatly folded them, and left them on the floor. Then she waited for his instructions.

"Fuck, you are perfection." Luca sat and stripped out of his shirt. "I need you next to me."

Flutters whispered through her, his praise making her wet and achy. He slid over, and she scooted in next to him. She rested her hands on his chest. "What do you want from me?"

"Tonight? Your company." He softly kissed her. "To sleep with you next to me."

"And tomorrow?"

"Your submission. In my dungeon, wet, moaning, and coming on my tongue."

She shivered as his fingers skirted across her abdomen.

"I need you, Mia." His eyes searched hers. "Tell me what *you* want."

Somehow, she knew if she wasn't honest, he'd take from her. He'd have her. Power radiated from him. She knew little about him except what her body craved. She was tired of fighting, fighting her needs, fighting her ideals, and tired of fighting this dangerous chemistry between them.

"Owned," she said. "I want to be owned. Submission isn't enough. A Dom with a whip isn't enough. You can make me come. But I'll only surrender to my Master."

***

Luca couldn't sleep. Mia slept in the bed, warm, naked, and tangled with him. After they'd eaten, he'd washed her beautiful body in the shower and then crawled into bed with her. Touching, tasting, never taking. Once sated, she'd instantly fallen asleep, her smooth thighs aligned with his.

They'd been in the air several hours. Outside the sun would be out, but the darkened blinds kept them cocooned in the intimate room. The scent of his shampoo lingered in her hair. He threaded his fingers through the soft tresses.

"Owned?"

Did she really understand what she asked?

Luca understood all too well the oppression of ownership. Unquestioning loyalty. One wasn't a member of the Bruno family without understanding the consequences of betrayal.

No one crossed Roberto Bruno, not even his sons.

"If I have to own you to have you, I will," he whispered. He only had to remember Giada's deceit to know he'd never trust in love again. That didn't mean Mia wouldn't be his.

His eyes finally closed, and he drifted into a fitful sleep, always aware of the woman next to him. And the dangerous family lair he lured her into.

***

When they were an hour out, Luca kissed Mia's shoulder. "We'll be landing soon."

She stretched, her back arched, and her ass nestled against his cock. "Hmm."

"I'm happy to stay in bed with you, but I need you to be presentable to my family. The airstrip is on the property." He slid his legs over the side of the mattress.

Soft with sleep, her gaze tracked him across the room. "Presentable?"

"Yes. There will be time to play tonight. Put on the dress."

She was quiet.

"Mia?"

"What is required for being presentable? A dress isn't going to cover the marks you've left on me. You brought me with you knowing what I am. My name doesn't change that." She glanced up into his face.

"You mistake my intention. Everyone will know who you belong to, want you, and wonder how I could have such a beautiful woman on my arm and in my bed."

She licked her lips.

"I haven't forgotten who you are, Mia. On the floor. On your knees." He grabbed his belt from the valet stand. "Arms behind you."

She knelt in front of him. He positioned behind her and belted her upper arms behind her back, forcing her breasts to thrust forward.

Standing in front of her again, he traced her lower lip with his thumb. With his other hand, he stroked his cock from base to tip. Pre-cum slicked the head. He painted her lips. When she slid her tongue against the slit, he raked his fingers into her hair and held her head immobile.

"Open."

Her lips parted, and he fed her his cock. She hummed her need for more, sucking him but unable to move with his hold on her.

Something felt off. The intimacy, the connection of last night morphed into a base need for a D/s exchange. A rush of anger surged through him. This wasn't the woman from last night. This was Tinker, a sub from the dungeon.

"Mia, look at me."

Her eyes pleaded for approval. As if he was entitled to her mouth and body simply because she was submissive and desperately sought a dominant who would understand her.

He'd had enough of Tinker. A strong, determined woman lurked beneath the surface. She was the one he wanted to own.

"Is this what you want? Tinker loves to suck cock." His voice lowered. "She's a pain slut in a dungeon. I watched her, watched her come all over the Professor's hand. Was it enough for him to rub the pain from your flesh after the lashes from the cane?"

Her eyes widened.

"Is it enough for you to see the bruises? Tinker is beautiful but doesn't see her true beauty."

She whimpered as he forced more of his cock into her mouth, then eased out.

"Tinker doesn't care who holds the whip so long as she hurts before she comes. Doesn't care if she's nurtured and protected by the one who leaves their mark."

Her tongue swirled over the length. His balls grew heavy. Heat and pressure ratcheted up his spine. His abdominals clenched as his orgasm encroached.

"Alex, the Professor." The names tasted bitter on his tongue. "Do they really care if you go home alone, knowing the gifts you offer are taken, never cherished?"

Her eyes closed, and tears slipped onto her cheeks.

"Tinker can't protect you, not from me. Tinker only exists in the club. You're here with me, and I know you feel for me, Mia. The same way I feel for you." Velvety hot suction pulled him deeper into her mouth. "Suck my cock because you belong to me."

He pumped his hips. Spit coated his dick and dripped from his balls.

Mia gagged. He inched back enough for her to catch her breath and then she greedily whimpered for more.

Luca fisted his cock, jerked from her mouth, and roared with his release. Hot ribbons of cum ejaculated onto her chest. Waves of euphoria washed over him, leaving him trembling and spent. He dropped to his knees, cupped her cheeks in his palms, and kissed her. Tongues tangled. He couldn't taste enough, couldn't express enough. She'd need more than his body and his dominance. She'd need to be convinced.

"I'm not interested in sharing Tinker with the dungeon," he said. "I am ruthless, Mia. Ruthless in my pursuits. Cruel to those who would take what is mine." His gaze narrowed as he freed her arms from the belt. "Be careful of what you ask for."

Her gaze hardened. She wiped her lips with the back of her hand. "I won't ask, Luca. It's up to you. I'm not more to you than anyone else, a pet to be played with in a dungeon." Her gaze traveled around the cabin of the plane. "Or a would-be lover in the bedroom of your private plane." She meshed her lips together, tasting the last of his essence. "I want to be owned. But I can't be bought. My virginity isn't for sale."

He sat back on his haunches, as if the sting of her words had slapped him. "Do you think I care about whether or not you'll let me fuck you?"

"Yes." Her head lowered. "I think you're seducing me, a perfectly played scene." She released a shuddering exhale. "Luca, I'm submissive. And you're more than I want to resist. But I'm not yours."

He tossed a towel to her feet. "Clean up, Tinker. I have a birthday party for my son."

***

Luca rested a hand on Mia's lower back as he escorted her from the plane. Acres of manicured gardens stretched from the landing strip to the rear of the mammoth property. Vineyards, rows of perfectly tended grapes covered the hills in the distance.

Armed gunman prowled the perimeter.

"Did you tell them you were bringing a guest?" Mia worried her lip between her teeth.

"No. But they don't get a say in who I'm involved with." Not anymore. "You look stunning."

"Presentable?"

"I didn't mean to make you feel you weren't. I only wish to protect you from the sharp eye of my family. You must know."

"Know what?"

"That you are the most beautiful woman I've ever seen." A loose braid tumbled over her shoulder, the blonde tresses a sharp contrast with the black dress hugging her curves. She wrapped a silk shawl around her shoulders, allowing it to drape into the crook of her arms.

"Papa!" Savio rushed down the slope, smiling, and waving his arms.

Luca bent and scooped up his son. He kissed his cheek and ruffled his dark hair.

"He looks just like you."

Luca smiled. "A family trait for all the Bruno men." He carried his son up the stone steps to the massive open patio. Sunlight glinted off the sparkling water in the two-tiered pool.

Savio rattled off a million and one questions and requests.

Luca slipped his hand into his pocket and pulled out a rare collector's coin.

Savio squealed. Luca set him down to run and show his cousins, family, and friends.

"He collects coins," he said to Mia. "I always bring him home one."

"That's sweet."

"That's Carlo. I don't know where he gets them, but he's always got my back, especially with Savio."

"Luca, you're late." Anna approached and hugged him.

"You look beautiful." Luca spoke in Italian and kissed his sister's cheeks but kept Mia close to his side. "My sister, Anna," he said in English. "This is Mia Toliver."

"Welcome, I'm so glad to see my brother looking happy," she said in Italian and kissed Mia's cheeks.

"She doesn't speak Italian."

Anna popped a hand on her hip. "Good, then I can tell you that you are fucking crazy bringing a woman to the party. Giada is going to cut her up and feed her to the sharks."

He kissed Mia's cheek and translated Anna's words. "She's happy you're here."

Mia snorted. "Does she speak English? Because I don't believe you but also tell her thank you considering I'm wearing her dress and shoes."

Anna's brow arched. "*My dress*?"

"I need a drink," he said.

Luca made introductions as he led Mia to the bar. Food filled the banquet tables. Wait staff mingled with the guests as they cleared dishes and refilled wine glasses.

"Are you okay?" he asked her.

"Overwhelmed. I don't belong here, Luca."

Sometimes he felt the same way. He handed her a glass of dark red wine. "From our vineyard."

She swirled the wine and then tipped the glass, letting the flavor float across her tongue. She took another sip. "Nice."

Luca leaned in and kissed her, sliding his tongue against hers for a taste. "Hmm. Agreed."

Mia bowed her head as a blush tinted her cheeks. "You're drawing attention to us."

"Then let me take you somewhere more private." He threaded his fingers with hers and led her into the house. "Come. I'll get you away from prying eyes for a minute."

"How many people live here?" She lifted her gaze to the cathedral ceilings.

Luca smiled. "I have no idea. The nanny, the chef, Carlo, Savio, of course. My brothers all have estates near here, but because of Savio, my family gathers here most of the time. Anna lives with my father. My mother passed when I was twelve."

He led her deeper into the house, away from the chatter and scrutiny of his family and guests. Their footfalls echoed in the empty corridor.

"Savio is raised by a nanny?" she asked.

He glanced to her. "No, he's raised by me." He swallowed, knowing he couldn't hide Giada from her. "I'm away often with business. His mother is here with him."

Mia slowed her steps. "You live with his mother?"

"Giada."

"So, you're still involved with her?" Mia took a step away from him.

"Yes, for Savio. A child should have both his parents."

She shook her head and rolled her eyes. "Then he probably shouldn't see his father with his arms around another woman."

Luca snagged her around the waist and pulled her close. "And why shouldn't he see his father happy? Giada is his mother. He needs her." He pulled back and stared hard into her eyes. "I don't. And she has even less need of me. My money, this is what she likes. I haven't lied to you."

"Luca." A voice echoed from down the corridor.

He tensed. He hated the way Giada spoke his name, a sultry seduction with a poison tongue. "She's here," he whispered to Mia.

Giada had always worn his money well. Petite like Mia but the similarities ended there. A cascade of dark curls fell to her waist. Flawless makeup, one high brow arched, and red painted lips twisted into a pasted smile. Fake lashes framed her hazel eyes. She crossed her arms under the full, round breasts he'd bought her after Savio was born.

"You're late for your son's birthday." She spoke in Italian as her gaze raked over Mia. "And you brought your current whore with you."

Luca released Mia's hand and took a menacing step toward Giada. "Better my whore, than my father's cunt."

She reached up to slap his face, but he grabbed her wrist.

"I see you still like it rough," she said.

"My likes are none of your concern." He dropped her wrist. "Behave, Giada. Go to our son. We have a birthday to celebrate."

She pressed her body close to his. "Don't fuck with me, Luca."

Luca's jaw clenched. "Do you think you can threaten me?"

"Don't push me because we both know I can do far more than threaten."

He gripped her shoulder and slammed her against the wall. "Then do it."

Her eyes widened. "One day…I will."

Luca stumbled back a few steps. "Get out." He barely spoke the words.

She pointed at Mia. "Keep her away from me and my son."

"My son," he roared.

"Luca?" He spun toward Mia. Her eyes darted wildly between him and Giada.

"Get the fuck out," he yelled to Giada.

"Welcome home," she spat in English. Then she turned and fled down the hall.

Luca raked his fingernails over his scalp. "Fuck!" He cursed and sent the vase of flowers on the hall table crashing to the floor. Porcelain splinters scattered across the tile.

A servant rushed from the other room. "*Signor* Bruno."

"My apologies." He spun away from the water spreading across the floor.

"Luca?" Anna appeared at the end of the hall.

"Take Mia to the party," he muttered.

Mia shook her head. "No. I don't want to go socialize…not without you. I shouldn't be here anyway."

He cupped her cheek. "Go with Anna. I'll see you later."

"Don't leave me with strangers," she said with a quiver in her voice.

"I wouldn't be kind to you," he whispered. He needed to vent his anger. He shifted his gaze to Anna. "Keep Giada away from her."

Anna stepped over the glass. "Come. We need wine and cake." She wrapped her arm around Mia's shoulder and led her down the hall.

Luca stormed from the room. He wrapped one hand over the other and cracked his knuckles. A fucking hour after bringing her into his lair, the lion had roared.

Chapter Four

Mia sat alone at a table as Anna went for cocktails. Music and laughter drifted on the warm afternoon air. Savio giggled, blowing bubbles as he ran between the legs of a tall gentleman.

Trying not to stare at the man who looked so much like Luca, she watched the ripples on the surface of the pool water. Tingles prickled the back of her neck. Her pulse raced.

"Aperol spritz," Anna said, setting two bright orange cocktails on the table. A slice of orange floated with ice cubes in the wide-mouth glass.

A man spoke beside them. Anna responded and the conversation continued in Italian. A shiver slipped along her spine. The deep voice, hard and with a dangerous edge, grated against her nerves. Suddenly, she wished she spoke Italian. She was sure the conversations centered around her.

"Mia Toliver, from America." Anna spoke in English. "She doesn't speak Italian." She smiled at Mia. "Our brother, Marco."

"Ah, a friend of Luca's." His voice softened but was no less intimidating. "Where is he?"

"Luca had a fight with Giada."

Marco laughed. "Our brother must take pleasure in receiving pain as much as he relishes giving it." His eyes rested on Mia. "Nothing changes between them. It's always hot or cold. He should learn to stay away from her."

"More like war or peace." Anna's gaze softened on Mia. "Luca would like peace. But she has a gift for making him angry." She sucked on the straw in her cocktail. "He should have known her nails were going to come out. She doesn't share well."

A lump welled in Mia's throat. She blinked against the pressure in her eyes. Giada wouldn't have to share. She'd get through the next couple of days and then get the fuck away from Luca Bruno.

Marco sat at the table. "Mia—"

"You can call me Tinker," she interrupted. There was no need to pretend she was anything else. She slipped the shawl from her shoulders. Let them stare. She wasn't ashamed of who she was.

Anna's gaze shifted to her bruises, but she didn't comment.

Marco's gaze raked over her, taking a slow slide over her breasts and lower.

The crowd of family and friends began to sing to Savio. "Luca should be here," Tinker said more to herself.

"He is." Anna lifted her gaze to the second-floor balcony. The wind caught Luca's bangs. He'd unbuttoned his shirt. The setting sun cast an amber glow on the white stone surrounding him. His eyes darkened, and his gaze narrowed. Tinker followed his line of sight.

Giada smiled and helped her son blow out his birthday candles. Luca lifted a drink to his lips and drank. His jaw clenched. She watched, waited for him to look for her, but his focus never wavered from Giada as she laughed and tugged a tendril of her beautiful dark hair from her lips. She squatted next to Savio and pointed to the balcony. The little boy waved, squealing his delight.

Tinker turned away. "Excuse me."

She stood from the table.

She wasn't sure where she was going, but she couldn't watch this. Pain ripped through her heart. Ruthless and cruel. He'd made her a player in his twisted game. Who had he meant to hurt more? Her or Giada?

Tinker weaved through the crowd and entered the house. Heading in the opposite direction of the balcony, she wandered down corridors. Unlike her cold and sterile prison, Luca's home revealed the comforts of family.

She entered the library. Beyond the colorful spines filling the shelves, paintings hung on the walls. Arched windows stretched the length of the far wall. Maroon curtains were tied back with black cords.

She stepped up to the glass. Parked cars lined the circular drive. More vehicles filled the flat grassy area beyond the stone border around the front of the property. Men with guns positioned as sentries.

She sank into the chair and tucked her legs under her. Quiet settled around her, but her thoughts couldn't let go of Luca. In a house this size, she could just disappear. Would he even notice her absence? She couldn't compete with the woman who stirred both his anger and his passion.

Perhaps she could appeal to Luca. She'd seen the dark need in his eyes when he looked at Giada. All he had to do was put Tinker on the jet and fly her home. She mentally chuckled. Maybe she could make an offer on his jet. She closed her eyes, settling deeper into the chair. Finally, her thoughts quieted, and her body released the building tension.

"Tinker," a soft, yet deep voice whispered to her. Strong fingers gripped her shoulders, and then softened as the touch cascaded along her arm. "Tinker."

She opened her eyes, momentarily disoriented. Her gaze snapped to the darkened windows. "Where am I?"

"In the library."

Her eyes focused on the man squatting in front of her. "Marco?"

A slow smile split his lips. "You must have fallen asleep. We've been searching for you. Luca is…he is concerned."

"Oh, I'm sorry." She stretched her aching legs.

"Don't be." His gaze roamed over her. "It's good for him."

Reality came rushing back. Would Marco help her? She had to get away from Luca. For the same reasons she'd come with him, she desperately needed to get away. "I need to leave," she whispered. "I don't want to interfere. He and Giada—"

"Nothing you do will change Luca and Giada. They hate each other."

"Hate is a powerful yet passionate emotion." She clasped her hands in her lap.

"Yes, for me." His wicked grin hinted at danger. His eyes so much like Luca, but older and somehow more menacing. Marco simmered with barely banked control. She swallowed, tamped down her fear, and tried to put space between them. While Luca made her shiver with need, Marco made her nervous.

"Anna told me what happened earlier. The Bruno men have tempers." He touched her braid, and then he grazed his knuckles over the bruises on her upper arms. "And we're possessive."

She shifted, uncomfortable with the touch. Uneasiness tightened her chest. The room had grown dark. They were alone. Icy fear slipped through her veins. She struggled to take a breath with her racing heart.

"But I can see you belong to Luca."

She didn't, but she stayed quiet.

"Giada believes Luca will always be hers. And because of Savio, Luca will never let her go. You will have to accept her in his life if you are going to be with my brother." He stood and held his hand out to Tinker.

She rose without touching him.

Marco closed the space between them. His fingers danced across her décolletage. "When he dresses you in her clothes, he's only going to provoke her more."

"I thought the dress belonged to Anna." She ran her hands over her hips.

"No. But it looks better on you." His gaze raked over her again. "Fucking Luca. Come, I'll take you to him."

Tinker walked next to him. She shifted her gaze to his imposing presence next to her. Her mouth grew moist, not from the breadth of his shoulders or the taper of his back. A leather harness wrapped his trim waist, the butt of the gun tucked against his left hip.

"Mia," Luca said with a gasp and stalked toward her.

"Found her asleep in the library." Marco tugged her braid. "See you later, Tinker."

He cocked a brow at his brother and walked away.

"Tinker?" Luca curled his hands into fists.

"You dressed me in her clothes," she hissed and grabbed the hem of her dress. She lifted it, but

Luca was faster. He grabbed her and pinned her arms behind her back.

"Not here. After the way my brother had his eyes on you, do you think I'd let him see you strip?" He backed her against the wall. "He touched you."

"Have you touched Giada? Or won't she let you?"

She pressed his hand to her breast. "You'll need to use your imagination. Her tits are bigger than mine."

Luca grabbed her hand and dragged her down the hall. She stumbled attempting to keep up. He jerked open a door and shoved her into the room. The door slammed closed.

Tinker yanked the dress over her head and threw it at his feet. She heaved a breath. "I want to go home."

"No." He locked the bedroom door.

"You want Mia. Here she is. Get me a fucking phone. I'll be off your property in thirty minutes."

He chuckled as he unbuttoned his shirt. "And how would you do that?"

"None of your business."

Luca shrugged out of his shirt.

A tingle started in her belly, growing hotter and slowly radiating through her limbs. "You think you're tough with your money and guns."

She needed to shut her mouth. Fiery accusations poised at the tip of her tongue. Money and guns were part of Mia's daily life.

"If I have to chain you to the wall in my dungeon, I will. But we are going to settle this." He unbuckled his belt, the clink of the metal an intimidating reminder of her vulnerability. The slide of leather teased her ears as it slid from his pants.

Tinker swallowed, adrenaline heating her blood.

Luca folded over the belt in his hand. "Giada is a cunt who slept with my brother and, I suspect, fucked my father. I'd cut off my dick before I'd stick it in her again."

Tinker swallowed her anger. "Your father and your brother? That's why Marco says you hate her?"

"Don't. I don't want your pity. I have my son. He's my responsibility. So yes, Giada is part of the package. I will provide for her. But I'll never share my bed with her." He sighed. "And I don't hate her. To hate, you have to be emotionally invested. I'm not. Unless she's standing in front of me, I rarely think of her. When she is in front on me, yes, she is usually a fucking thorn in my side. I accept this for Savio."

With the belt at his side, he pointed to the bed. "Bend over, Mia."

"Call me Tinker."

Tension rolled from him in waves. He closed the space between them. "You've questioned me at every turn, accused me of betraying you, and allowed my brother to put his hands on you. Bend over the bed, ass in the air, and count the licks of my belt. This is your punishment."

"I didn't allow Marco to touch me." She should hate this, but she couldn't. Emotions, a welling of need, built within her. The powerful set to his jaw, the command in his voice, and the flex of muscle in his arms had her trembling.

Luca spun her around and bent her over the bed. "Did you tell him no?" Instead of striking her with the belt, he braced his hand on her back and slid his fingers through her soaked folds. "What is it, Mia? The thought of the belt? Or does fighting with me make you hungry for discipline?"

She was wet the moment he'd touched her in the hall. Powerless over his pull on her, she simply slid into her role as submissive. His possessiveness scared her because it's all she'd ever wanted from a Dom.

"Answer me."

"Yes, Sir." His voice sent a shiver over her flesh. "It's you, Luca. You make me wet."

"Count them, Mia."

"Tinker."

He raised his arm. "The first two are for arguing, *Mia*. Tell me to call you Tinker again and it will be three." The loop of the belt snapped against her buttocks.

Mia—Tinker—No, for him she would be Mia.

"One," she said on an exhale.

Another stinging lash striped her. She trembled. "Two."

"For questioning my loyalty."

She cried out as the belt branded her flesh. She did question his loyalty. But she wasn't at Protocol, and she wasn't his…not yet.

"Three," she whispered. Red-hot heat burst under the skin.

She braced for the final strike. Instead, cool air blew against her flesh.

"Sir?"

"Shh." He blew against the reddening welts, then he leaned in and licked her pussy.

Mia clutched fistfuls of the bedding. She rose onto her tiptoes as his tongue danced over her folds. Luca stood, flipped her to her back, and pressed her knees to her shoulders.

Her gaze locked with his. "Please."

"Ah, sweet Mia. It's my turn to say please." He latched onto her clit and sucked. She gripped her knees and opened wider. He licked, tasted, and nibbled. His tongue curled into her opening, drawing more of her essence into his mouth. "Come for me."

Mia fought an inner battle. She rode the edge, ready to tumble over. She could let go, fall into the swirling waters of ecstasy, but her heart wouldn't let her. A missing piece needed filled.

She shivered, violent trembles racking her body. "I can't," she pleaded, jack-knifing upright. "Luca—" She could feel the terror in her mind and hear it in her voice.

"Mia, *amore.*"

She clung to him, banding her arms around his thick shoulders, and resting her forehead on his chest. She couldn't watch him love another woman. "If she still holds your heart, let me go."

"My heart is black, Mia. But my desire is only for you."

Taking his hand, she pressed it to her neck. His fingers collared her throat. "I need you to touch me."

Slowly dragging his touch lower, gliding over her breast, down her quivering belly, until his fingers touched her intimately, grazing her clit.

"Inside me."

"No, Mia. You're not ready. Not like this. Not after anger."

Yes, just like this, when only raw honesty remained between them. They'd both shared, become vulnerable.

"I need more." She spread her thighs. An empty ache needed filled. "I need you."

Luca slid his finger into her passage. She moaned at the slight stretch. Inner muscles contracted on the invasion.

"You're so small, so tight." He slid his finger out then pressed in again.

Her thighs snapped together, the sensation overwhelming her.

"Kiss me," he demanded.

Mia slid her mouth against his, opening and aggressively tangling her tongue with his. A riot of sensations surged through her. He curled his finger, sliding in and out of her center. With his other hand, he fondled her breast, pinching her nipple.

"Luca," she begged. "I want you." She wanted inside his black heart the same way he was forcing his way into hers.

"Nothing you will regret tomorrow." He pumped his finger faster, rubbing her wet, achy walls. Flashes of light sparked behind her eyes. Inner muscles contracted. Another twist inside of her and she shattered. Her body convulsed as she milked his finger and cream slicked her passage.

Mia gasped for breath, her pulse racing.

Luca hissed as her nails, like talons, clawed his shoulders. Her hips rolled, bucking against his hand.

"*Bellissima*," he whispered against her lips. He pulled her close, holding her trembling body, and brushed a tear from her cheek. "Are you okay?"

She lowered her gaze and shook her head. "I'm hungry."

***

Luca sat across from Mia in the kitchen. Warmth simmered in his gut. They'd raided the refrigerator. Leftover food from the birthday party covered the giant island in the center of the room.

Mia popped a meatball into her mouth and hummed in pleasure as she chewed. Then she licked sauce from the pad of her thumb. "You're staring at me."

"I like to see you eat." He smiled as he layered meat and cheese on a cracker. "And I should have dressed you in my clothes on the plane. This is much better."

She wore his dress shirt. The tails barely covered her ass, and she'd left most of the buttons undone. The hour had grown late, and the house was quiet. "I'm sorry about earlier, about being bratty."

"Something tells me you're not too sorry."

"It's hard to be sorry when the punishment feels so good."

Luca shifted to the seat next to her and spun her stool in his direction. "And the other, the reward?" With a fork, he cut into the birthday cake and brought it to her lips.

"Sweet." She closed her mouth over the cake and slid her lips along the fork. She hummed and swallowed.

Luca kissed her, tasting the seam of her lips and gliding his tongue along hers. "Delicious."

He pulled her onto his lap, her pussy riding the ridge of his erection. This time she took the fork and fed him a bite. As he chewed, she rested her hands on his shoulders and ground against him.

"Why only three lashes of the belt?"

"Because you didn't earn the fourth. You didn't allow Marco to touch you." He pressed his lips to her. "He wanted you."

"I know."

Luca stilled.

"But I want you." She kissed him. "Only you."

His fingers tangled in her hair. She moaned, rocking her hips. With his forearm, he cleared a space and lifted her onto the counter.

She leaned back on outstretched arms. He smeared frosting over her clit, bent his head, and licked her clean. He slid into her heat, the tightness of her pussy closing around his finger.

Mia cried out, her hand sliding into the cake. Her gaze met his as she sucked her fingers like she sucked his cock, thrusting them into her mouth, tasting the cake, and slowly pulling them from her lips. She moaned and dragged her tongue along the outside of her palm, curling around her pinky, licking the frosting.

Mastering her body, he speared his tongue into her, feasting on her cream.

"Luca," she breathed his name, careening toward release.

"You don't need permission when we're not in the dungeon. Come for me, *bella*." He buried his face between her legs, drinking in her arousal, and relishing her surrender to pleasure.

She jolted, quaking under his mouth. Her raspy breaths filled the quiet kitchen. He continued to lick her until the final flutters settled against his tongue.

A coy smile found her lips. He enjoyed this teasing side of her. Playful, aroused, and almost happy. Tinker kept Mia in a controlled box. But alone together, Mia's guard was slowly coming down.

"I see your thoughts hard at work." He sipped her lips.

"My thoughts aren't hard at all." She palmed his cock.

Luca moved his hands out of the way as she opened his trousers. Since they'd only dressed in the essentials, he hadn't worn underwear. His trousers dropped to the floor.

She slid from the counter and knelt on the floor. She opened her mouth and glided her lips along the length.

"Fuck," he said as a plea.

Soft, moist tissue of her mouth clung to his flesh. As she pumped his shaft with her fist, she pressed against the frenulum with the tip of her tongue, tracing the ridges and valleys. She gently cupped his balls, tugging the sac, and rolling her fingers under, against the taint.

His buttocks clenched. Saliva glistened on her lips. Slurping sounds blended with the heaviness of his breaths. He closed his eyes and combed his fingers through her hair.

"*Bella*," he growled.

A creak sounded from the far side of the room. Marco cupped his cock, watching Mia.

Luca narrowed his gaze. "Get the fuck out."

Mia sucked harder, moaned louder.

Luca lost the edge. Heat streaked along his spine. His balls drew up and his gut clenched. He thrust into Mia's mouth as hot spurts of cum jetted through his dick and splashed her throat.

She reached between her legs with her free hand and toyed with her clit. As she sucked the last of his release, she plowed into another of her own. Like a violent storm, she shivered, shuddered, and finally sagged against his thighs.

Luca lifted his gaze. Marco was gone. What the fuck was he still doing here in his house? Probably enjoy Giada's pleasures.

He pulled up his pants, scooped Mia into his arms, and headed back to his bedroom.

"What about the mess?" she said, resting her head on his shoulder.

"That's why I have a staff." He carried her to the bed and set her down. He slipped the two buttons loose and peeled the shirt from her body. Naked, he climbed in next to her.

She curled into him. He wrapped his arms around her and kissed her temple. "Good night, Mia."

"Tinker," she whispered and smiled.

With her warm body pressed against his, Luca relaxed. His eyes closed. The soft sounds of her breathing lulled him into a restful slumber. He hadn't realized he'd fallen asleep until a light knocking on the door woke him.

Before he could respond, Carlo filled the doorway.

During the night, the sheet had fallen to the floor. Mia slept on her stomach, her beautiful body on display, including the red welts from her punishment.

Carlo glanced at her but quickly averted his eyes. "We have an issue."

Luca flipped the sheet over her and covered his cock. "Give me two minutes."

He nodded and stepped from the room.

Luca crossed to the closet and grabbed a pair of sweats. He scrubbed his hands over his head.

Carlo leaned against the wall in the hallway, an unlit cigarette dangling from his lips. He pulled it from his mouth and tucked it behind his ear.

"Greco got pinched."

"Fuck." Greco was a made man for the family—an earner. He worked in banking and was able to pass off questionable transactions with little scrutiny.

"Roberto says he's your man. Wants to know if you want a button man to clip him before he has the chance to break."

No, he didn't want him taken out—not yet. But the situation needed to be monitored.

"Greco won't rat the family out." But that didn't mean they were without risk. "He knows we can get to him anywhere. Send Barone in. He has friends in the Ministry of Justice. He'll remind Greco where his loyalties lie."

Carlo stuck the cigarette back in his mouth and lit it. His brows furrowed. "You need to wrap up your business with Ferraro. He sniffs the wind and catches this, you know he'll pull out."

Luca wasn't stupid. His business with Alex was a hundred percent legal. Fuck, nothing was one hundred percent. But legitimate business gave camouflage for less ethical endeavors.

"One more thing," he said to Carlo. "I fucked up with Mia."

He chuckled. "Seeing her ass, I'd assume she was the one who fucked up." He blew out a stream of smoke.

"That was all consensual."

"Kinky motherfucker."

"Yeah, well, go get her some clothes. She wears the same size as the bitch."

Carlo chuckled as he pushed away from the wall. "She must have behaved yesterday if she's been upgraded from cunt to bitch."

"Giada behave?"

"Yeah, never would've worked between you two. She wouldn't let you paddle her ass."

"Get the clothes." Luca turned and entered the bedroom.

Mia still slept. Blonde hair fanned against the pillow. Smooth flesh stretched across the sheets. He stripped out of the sweats, slid in next to her, and drank in her warm scent.

He sighed, relaxing against her. The softness of her form molded to the firm contours of his. In the fucked up, crazy world he lived in, she was the one thing that made sense.

A couple hours later, she stirred against him. She stretched, arching her back against his groin, yawned, and rolled to her side.

"Morning." She slid her fingers beneath the sheet and curled her fingers around his shaft.

Luca kept his eyes closed as she squeezed his dick.

"Do we have plans for today?" She pumped her fist, slow and steady, with a firm grip, then gathering fluids from the slit, teased the head.

"Ask me after I come." He bent one knee and flicked the sheet from his body. She pumped faster, squeezing and teasing until his gut clenched and cum shot from his dick, splashing his belly.

As his breathing returned to normal, he wiped his cum from his chest with the sheet. "Good morning." Leaning over, he kissed her forehead. "I need a shower."

He slid from the bed and strode toward the ensuite bathroom. He glanced over his shoulder.

Mia curled into the pillow, her gaze tracking him.

"You can sleep, or you can join me."

She smiled and scrambled from the bed.

Luca laughed, almost not recognizing the sound coming from him. He couldn't remember the last time the pressure of his work hadn't suppressed any glimmer of happiness from his life.

Now he was laughing. All because of her.

***

Luca sat across from Mia on the bedroom balcony. She wore his bathrobe, a towel wrapped turban style around her head, and a steaming cup of coffee in her hands. She had one leg bent on the chair, her gaze focused on the distant cliffs and the water below.

"You're staring," she said, taking a sip of coffee.

"You're beautiful. Do you take after your mother?"

She bowed her head. "Strangely, no. I don't look like my mom or my dad." A sad smile tilted her lips. "I look like my brother. But I'm not sure if that means I have more masculine features or if he could have passed for a girl if he put on a bit of makeup and grew his hair out."

Nothing about her was masculine.

"You haven't mentioned your brother." Considering his three, specifically Marco, had descended on her.

She squinted into the morning sunshine. "I don't talk about him." Her gaze dropped to the steaming cup of coffee. "It hurts too much."

She took a sip.

"Family can be hard," he said.

"I know."

"Mia?"

She turned to him.

"Talk to me."

Silence stretched between them. Luca leaned back in his chair and closed his eyes, letting the sun warm his face. She would talk when she was ready. He didn't have to wait long.

"He died three years ago."

He glanced to her.

She set her coffee cup on the table, pulled both of her knees into her chest, and wrapped her arms around her shins. "He was my best friend. Sometimes my only friend." She smiled with her memories. "We grew up…sheltered. Maybe that's what made him overprotective." A dejected laugh spilled from her lips. "More than overprotective. He was an ass. But he was two minutes older, so he thought that made him the boss."

"Twins."

She nodded and rested her forehead on her knees, her eyes filled with unshed tears. "When he died, I died."

Luca stood from his chair, picked her up, and settled back in his chair with her on his lap. He held her as silent tears slipped onto her cheeks. Once she started, it was as if the dam burst, and she couldn't stop.

"We'd lost our parents. A horrible…accident," she choked on the words. "We were always alone. But once they were gone, I lost him, too."

He simply held her, his arms around her with his hands still. She trembled as she spoke, the words becoming whisper quiet.

"I can't imagine what he went through." She audibly swallowed. "He wouldn't talk to me." Her voice broke. "We were twins. Shouldn't I have known something was wrong? We'd had a funeral for my parents. I don't think either one of us could really understand how there could be nothing left to bury."

Fuck. His grip tightened. "*Mi dispiace*. I'm sorry, Mia."

She shrugged one shoulder. "Sometimes, I think maybe it was easier I mean, they just never came home." She tilted her head back, her hands curled into fists. "Why did he do it?" she wailed. "How could he leave me alone? Leave me with all this shit inside."

Fear squeezed his chest. "Mia?"

She struggled to stand, but he held her tighter.

"You're not alone." He pressed his lips to her shoulder. "I'm here."

"I'm broken," she said. "He was a part of me." With her eyes closed, more tears spilled onto her cheeks. "I found him."

He touched her cheek, forcing her to look into his eyes. "It's okay to be angry."

"I'm not angry." She traced the dark hairs on his chest with her fingertips. "I miss him. I want to remember when we were good. But when I think about him, the only thing I see is the day—" She pressed her lips to his. "Tell me something good. I don't want to talk about him now. I want to be with you."

"I want to take you somewhere special today." He tugged the towel from her head and sifted his fingers through the damp tendrils of her hair. He loved the blonde color and the soft feel of it. Almost as much as he loved the texture of her skin. Sliding his hand into the robe, he touched her warm flesh.

A knock sounded on the bedroom door.

"*Prego entra*," Luca hollered, inviting the person into the room. "Perfect timing."

He lifted her from his lap. With his thumbs, he dried her tears. Lacing their fingers, he led her into the bedroom.

Carlo entered the room with his arms full of shopping bags.

Anna skipped in behind him, squealing with excitement, and with more bags draped from her arm. "Shopping for you, Mia."

"What is this?" Mia asked Luca.

He tugged on the robe's belt, parting the panels. "I want to dress you."

She glanced over her shoulder to Carlo and Anna, and she smiled. Then she wound her arms around Luca's neck. "You know I don't mind an audience."

She dropped her arms, and the robe slipped from her body.

"Out," he barked to Carlo and Anna.

Carlo laughed.

Anna huffed. "I want to see her in the clothes." She braced her hands on her hips. "You can have a fashion show later."

Mia laughed.

Luca kissed her nose. "Spend time with Anna. I'll be back in an hour." He grabbed a plain black T-shirt and stretched it over his head. Then he covered her mouth with his and kissed her, a thorough, sweeping possession with lips and tongue. He smiled and smacked her ass. "Be good."

***

Mia pulled the robe back on and sat on the edge of the bed. Anna pulled clothes from the bags.

Mia peered into a bag filled with panties and bras. She lifted a scrap of black lace.

Anna wagged her brows.

"Did you pick this out?" Mia asked.

"No. I only helped carry the bags in from the car. But I snooped. Carlo did the shopping. He does whatever Luca asks of him." She pulled a black corset from another bag. "Oh my god. My brother will love this, but I don't think he'll love that Carlo picked it out."

Mia laughed. "I think Carlo has seen more than either of us would like to think about."

Anna arched a brow. "I wouldn't have said anything, but I know my brother plays hard—rough. But then I watch him with Savio, and he's so gentle and kind, even after everything that happened with Giada. She just keeps dragging him back into her hell."

Mia's chest tightened. "Maybe he still cares for her. They have Savio."

Anna held up a pair of tapered jeans. "I don't understand any of my brothers." She tossed the jeans to her. "Try them on."

All the tags had been cut from the clothing. Mia stepped into the jeans and pulled them over her hips.

"You should wear those." Anna sat on the edge of the bed. "I haven't seen my brother smile in a long time." She fished through another bag. "Stefano and Orlando are always together. Chasing girls, gambling, you know, being rich, attractive playboys. Marco and Luca, they are the same. Always working." She held up an elegant off the shoulder dress. "Oh, this is gorgeous. Carlo is going back to the village. I need this dress."

Mia smiled. "Take it. Luca will never know."

Anna dropped the dress. "Ah, no. You don't take anything that belongs to Luca." She arched a brow. "I think you know this. I see the way he looks at you."

But what about Giada? She thought back over the things he'd said. They had history, volatile history. But she believed him. Without knowing Luca well, she had no doubt that once betrayed, forgiveness wouldn't be easy. The insecurity coiling in her gut eased.

"He says he's taking me somewhere special. Jeans and a top or the dress?"

Anna's lips pursed. "If you wear the dress, he's going to have his hands where they don't belong in public. But since you seem to shed your clothing easily, I don't think so much you'll mind."

Mia stripped out of the jeans, standing naked in front of Anna. She chose the scrap of lace black panties and opted not to wear the matching bra.

The royal blue dress fit to perfection, off the shoulder on one side and two panels of fabric draping her body to just below the knee and hanging lower in the back. The panels overlapped in the front, creating a slit from mid-thigh down.

In another bag, she found a couple of pairs of shoes. Carlo chose well. The colors and styles would mix and match with the clothing. Too bad she'd only be here for a day or two more.

"We should go find Luca," Anna said.

"Almost ready." Mia went to the bathroom, braided her hair, and just as she had yesterday, used Luca's toothbrush to brush her teeth. She slipped on soft leather, beige mules, and picked up the designer sunglasses for later. "Carlo has excellent tastes."

Anna looked her over with an appreciative eye. "I think we would all say Luca does."

"Thank you." She smoothed her hands over her hips and went to find the man with a dangerous need to own more than her submission.

As they passed the kitchen, Mia blushed.

A woman mopped the floor. Their eyes connected, but rather than a critical glare, the woman's lips pulled into a teasing smile.

Anna spoke to the woman in Italian.

"He's on the patio with Marco."

Mia slipped on the sunglasses as she approached. Luca hadn't noticed her. He and Marco seemed to be in a heated conversation. Marco leaned back in a chair, watching Savio splash in the pool. Luca paced, his arms doing as much talking as the words flying from his lips.

Anna stopped and put her hand on Mia's arm. "It's not a good time."

"What are they saying?"

She turned Mia around and headed back toward the house. "Ah, just work, family. Let's give them a few minutes, *sì*?" She led Mia to a small table and chair where she could see the patio. "Wait, I'll see how long."

Mia nodded, uncomfortable, but not upset. She was a stranger to them. Luca hadn't exactly been hiding that family business might entail more than a vineyard and international holdings.

The woman in the kitchen brought Mia a cup of coffee and a pastry.

"*Grazie*." Mia sipped the coffee and nibbled the sweet bread.

Outside, Anna appeared to be giving her brothers a good ass chewing. Both men had grown quiet. Anna pointed from Savio to the house. Great, Mia did not want to be dragged into family drama.

Luca threw up his hands. He said something to Anna because she grabbed a towel and hurried to Savio. Luca stormed across the patio, and by the time he approached her, the hard line of his mouth had softened.

"Ready?" he asked.

Mia stood. "I think you might be needed here."

"Today, I'm yours." He checked his watch. "But we'll need to hurry."

He led her through another part of the house she'd never seen. At the end of the hall, they took an elevator to the lower floor. He was quiet, his hands stuffed into his pockets and tired lines creased his eyes. The doors opened to an underground garage.

As he passed a wall of fobs, he selected a key ring with a golden bull on a black base. With the push of a button, the doors on the sports car lifted.

He held her hand as she sank into the cockpit-style, leather, bucket seat. The door lowered as he went around to the driver's side. Once in the vehicle, he turned his heated gaze to her. "You look stunning."

Inside, she turned to jelly, and shivers slithered over her flesh. Unsure of how to respond, she slipped on the sunglasses. Because what she really wanted to say was *please*.

The engine squealed and then rumbled into a high-powered purr. Luca drove out of the parking garage, hit the gas, and fired down the isolated street leading away from the house.

The engines roared as they rounded a bend. Mia held her fluttering stomach and laughed. His hand reached across the console and settled on her thigh.

The laughter became a moan as his fingers grazed her inner thigh and tunneled under the slit in the dress.

"Fuck," he cursed and grabbed the steering wheel with both hands. The car cornered around another bend in the road. "I guess I should focus on my driving."

They drove in silence for a few minutes.

"Is everything okay with Marco?"

A muscle ticked in his jaw. "I don't always agree with my brother but he's the underboss. He listens, but right now, he has his head up his ass." He glanced to her and smiled. "I wanted today, just for us."

They drove into the lot of the marina and parked.

"Sailing?"

"Yes, and wine tasting." Reaching beneath the seat, he produced a gun. He checked the chambers and slid the gun into the holster at his waist.

"Luca?"

"It's nothing to worry about." The hard line of his mouth returned. Tension bunched the muscles of his arms.

She folded her hands in her lap. "I'm not asking you to explain."

They both had secrets they weren't ready to share.

"I want you alone. You would prefer to have Carlo with us?"

"No, just don't mix your business with our pleasure. And don't shoot anyone when I'm around." She'd had enough death in her life, having lived and lost too much. When bad men did bad things, sometimes the dangerous men of the world had to even the score. Time with Luca had shown her that he wasn't just Alex's business associate. The Bruna family were Mafia.

Luca exited the vehicle and opened the door for her. "Are you upset?"

"Am I upset that there are parts of your life you can't share with someone you've only known a week? No."

"If we decide that we want more?"

She couldn't think about that. If he shared his secrets, he'd expect hers. She wasn't ready, and she might not ever be ready to tell him everything.

"We have today," she said. "Just for us."

He held her hand and escorted her to the sailboat. Two men tightened the lines. They spoke to Luca in Italian. Both were huge men, muscles straining the tight black T-shirts with the Bruno lion logo on the breast pockets.

"They're ready," he said and helped her to the center seating section of the seventy-foot sailboat. "Once we get out to sea, I'll give you the tour."

Mia leaned back on the cushion. Luca gave each of the men a hug with a thud to their back with his fist. They spoke in quieter tones, nodding, and checking the time.

Luca returned to her side. He stripped off his gun and tucked it into the compartment next to her.

Salty wind tickled her lips as the boat cut through the water. Once they were away from the marina and heading out to see, the crew began shouting.

Luca jumped from one side of the sailboat to the other, working the riggings. Cranks turned and masts swung across the bow of the ship. Wind caught the sail, unfurling the beautiful, white headsail emblazoned with the Bruno family crest.

Laughter poured from the crew as the sailboat picked up speed. Lines were secured. The boat bounced on waves, creating a mist of water along the side.

Mia slipped off her shoes and stretched her legs along the bench. One bent leg parted the split in her dress. With a hand resting between her thighs, she kept the wind from lifting her dress and exposing her panties. Her other arm draped over her head.

She closed her eyes and listened to their beautiful Italian voices. Luca's rich laughter made her heart flutter. He sounded happy, content to be working with his crew. A drastic difference in the tone he'd had with Marco on the patio.

A shadow blocked the sun. Using her hand as a visor, she squinted into the face of the man standing over her.

"You look good on my sailboat."

She twisted to sit up. "So do you."

He had stripped off his shirt. Sunlight glinted off the sheen of sweat on his torso. "Come." He held her hand and led her to the cabin below deck.

A sailboat this size would typically have living quarters, but the interior had been converted to host dinners and wine tasting events. However, a bunk style couch stretched across the back of the room.

He opened the clear door to the temperature-controlled wine rack and ran his fingers across the labels until finding the one he wanted.

"We only serve wine from our vineyards," he said. "This is one of my favorites."

Luca grabbed two chilled wine glasses with the lion head etched into the glass. As he poured, the vibrant red wine swirled into the glass.

"Enjoy."

Her fingers brushed his as she accepted the glass. Anticipation slithered over her. She licked her upper lip as she lifted the glass. His eyes darkened. She took a sip, letting the flavor float across her palate.

"*Perfetto*," she said.

He laughed and filled his glass. "Ready?"

She nodded.

Taking the bottle with them, Mia followed Luca topside. He grabbed his discarded shirt before they carefully made their way to the bow of the ship. He slipped the bottle into a holder along the rail.

Low side-by-side deck chairs were anchored to the boat. She sat and stretched her legs out in front of her. He shrugged his shirt back on before sitting in the chair next to her.

"I love this," he said. Wind whipped around them as the sailboat cut through the turquoise waters. "I used to imagine sailing out to sea and never returning. I wanted to escape my life." He angled toward her. "But I have responsibilities to my family. Responsibilities I will never walk away from. I would do anything to protect those important to me."

Mia searched his eyes. "You can try. But sometimes the choices aren't yours to make. People make bad decisions. Sometimes there's collateral damage."

"Do you speak from experience?" He laced his fingers with hers, leaned back, and closed his eyes.

She pulled her fingers away. "I'm sure even you've made decisions you've regretted."

He turned to her. "And some, such as having you here with me now, I'll never regret." With the wind gusting over them, he closed his eyes again.

Mia stared at his profile. A scar marred his cheek just below his temple. She traced the faint line with her fingertip. "What happened here?"

"Life. Teenage boys getting into mischief. Orlando was a bad influence on me and Stefano."

She'd briefly met Orlando at the birthday party. "Something tells me it's not Orlando who is the bad influence."

He laughed.

"You're still a bad influence."

"We both know I can be persuasive." He opened his arms, indicating he wanted her on his lap.

Shifting over, she straddled him. The split in her dress gapped as her thighs spread and she settled against his cock. "Can I kiss you, Sir?"

Luca leisurely slid his lips against hers, gliding his tongue along the seam and slipping inside for a taste. He groaned as he braced his hands on her hips, holding her flush to his groin.

For a moment, it felt as if they were the only two people on earth. The sound of the water against the hull blended with the cool mist spraying over the bow. His hands roamed over her back, her bare shoulder, and along her ribs as he continued to kiss her. Tongues touched and tangled. Lips meshed and sipped into a dance between tender seduction and intense possession.

"I wanted us to have this time," he said, "without the distraction of my family, and for you, outside of Protocol."

"I admit, had you told me your intentions, I would've said no." And she would have missed out on seeing the different facets of the dominant man who demanded her obedience and touched her body with passionate kisses and fiery caresses.

"Do you regret saying yes?"

She dipped her head, but he lifted her chin.

"No." But she couldn't bring herself to say more.

Luca waited for a few beats of her heart. "If you haven't yet realized it, you will. You're mine now. Tell me."

"I worry I'll regret not saying yes to more."

"Luca," one of the crew hollered.

He lurched forward, setting her to the side. "We should go below for our lunch," he said as he stood.

Mia watched as the crew began working the lines. "What are they doing?"

"Spilling the wind. We need to slow the boat." The sails started to flap in the wind and the boat quickly lost momentum. "Please, go below and wait for me."

In the distance, a speedboat approached. Fear streaked along her spine from the palpable tension between Luca and the crew. Her heart raced. Mia kept her footing as she hurried toward the cockpit of the boat.

Luca retrieved his gun from the seating compartment before following her down the companionway and going below to the dining area. He checked the chamber, then slid the gun into the holster.

"What's going on, Luca?"

He kissed her hard and fast. "Just a little business. Please, stay below." He hesitated, then opened a cupboard and grabbed another handgun. "Have you ever fired a gun?"

She swallowed hard, wanting to scream at him. Panic ripped through her. Had she ever handled a gun? No! She had armed guards.

"Mia!"

She snapped her gaze to his. "No, I've never handled a gun. Luca, what have you done?"

He didn't have to say anything. He'd brought her back into the world she'd escaped, back into the world that had destroyed her life. He offered both her survival with BDSM, and her demise with the underworld she could no longer deny.

***

The sailboat heaved-to, the sails working against each other to keep the boat steady. They'd sailed a little more than twelve kilometers off the coast into international waters.

Lorenzo and Carmine were two of Stefano's best. Semi-automatic rifles crossed their torso. Carmine took a position to give him the advantage over the men approaching in the speedboat. Lorenzo held the wheel.

This was Stefano's exchange, but he'd been tasked with seeing to Barone and the Greco situation. Since that was technically Luca's issue, Marco had decided Luca could do the pickup.

Marco had expected Luca to leave Mia behind. A ploy to get her alone, away from Luca. Luca refused.

Carmine glanced through the binoculars. He hollered to Lucas, confirming the identities of the men in the boat. "Four men, one starboard, two aft, and the driver. Semi-automatics." Carmine continued to call out his visual assessment.

Luca grabbed another gun from the storage next to the captain's chair at the wheel. He slid it against his back at the waistband of his jeans. Before he moved to meet the men, he glanced over his shoulder to the companionway.

Mia watched, her arms at her side, and her hands clasped in front of her. The color had drained from her face, and her petite form seemed almost fragile.

"It's over in two minutes," he said to her.

The spark had faded from her eyes, and her quivering lips had thinned to a strained line. Tears filled her eyes. "Be careful."

"Nothing…no one touches her," he said to Lorenzo and Carmine in Italian.

"Diamonds are the only thing coming aboard," Carmine said with a laugh, his gun aimed and his finger next to the trigger.

The speedboat powered down the engines. Three of the men aimed their guns at Luca.

"Who the fuck are you?" one of the men in the speedboat asked.

Lorenzo stepped next to Luca, his rifle pointed at the man to the left, the one who appeared to be nervous next to the other three. Someone easily mistaken for an associate. "Jamal, is that how you address Stefano's brother Luca? I would hate for you to offend a member of the Bruno family."

"Would Stefano be offended if his cargo was handed over to the wrong person?"

Luca raised his hand, stopping Lorenzo. "Stefano was called away on family business."

The man's gaze shifted to Lorenzo. "When will I hear from Stefano?"

"How the fuck should I know? You have questions, ask the man standing right in front of you. That's who pays your fucking bill." He shifted his gun to the left two inches to put a bead on the guy at the wheel. "Move your hand another inch, and I'll feed you to the sharks."

The man slowly lifted his fingers, showing he had a cigarette. He lit the tip and inhaled.

"Stefano will be in touch whenever he decides is a good time," Luca said. "Now I've had my sails idle long enough. Hand over the package to Lorenzo or move along. If you have an issue, take it up with Stefano."

The man seemed to weigh his options. After the longest minute of Luca's fucking day, the man finally nodded to the associate smoking the cigarette. He tossed a black cinched bag to Lorenzo. To catch it he had to let go of his rifle.

Carmine shifted. Tension built. Lorenzo opened the pouch, ensured the content was expected and not a ruse to take out a member of the Bruno family, and then handed the bag to Luca.

Luca shook a few diamonds from the bag into his palm. Sunlight glinted off the rare conflict stones. Blood diamonds. Highly illegal and extremely profitable.

He'd been in much worse positions than facing guerrilla leaders who didn't know who the fuck he was. Guns, high value commodities, and unfamiliar players carried high risks. And he had a woman below deck that was going to expect an explanation. But how much did he tell her?

With a nod, he concluded the family business. The speedboat raced into the horizon. He left Lorenzo and Carmine to set the sails for speed and get them back to shore. He went to find Mia.

She sat in the corner of a small sleeping couch at the back of the room with a bottle of wine. She tipped the bottle to her lips.

"What year? If it's the twenty-sixteen, it was considered the near perfect year."

Luca opened the wine rack and selected a bottle from the lower rung. He twisted the bottom of the dark glass bottle where the seam of the cut flawlessly blended with the label. He took the pouch of diamonds, carefully tucked them into the hidden compartment, concealing them, and then screwed the bottle back together.

"Was I just a decoy for you?"

Once he returned the wine bottle to the rack, he pulled the gun from his waistband, and set it on the counter. "A decoy? No."

She tipped the bottle and drank several more swallows. "Why did you bring me out here? I know how this works." She closed her eyes and took several breaths. "I'm either a distraction or a decoy. I don't want to know what this shit was all about. Fuck you for making me think any of this was for us."

Luca grabbed the wine and set it to the side. "What do you think would have happened if those men attempted to come aboard?"

"You tell me."

"I'd have put a bullet in their head." He took a step toward her, but she flinched, shifting into the corner of the couch.

"What about Interpol? Or Italian police?" Her eyes locked on his.

He raked his fingers through his hair. "Fuck." She shouldn't have been here. He'd come home for a birthday party, not to drag—what was Tinker to him? Initially a sub in a dungeon. He'd have denied she was anything more than a challenge. And he'd be lying. She was all he wanted. Fuck the rest.

Perhaps the blame was his. If he brought her into the family business, he'd never let her go. But he hadn't wanted this, not today. Not like this.

What the fuck did Marco think would happen? He wasn't going to leave her at the house alone. Not with his brother salivating at the sight of her. For Marco women were temporary, good for sex, and when needed, useful to the family.

Mia wasn't Giada. Mia wouldn't betray him with his brother. But he had no intention of leaving her alone with a man intent on conquest. Luca protected what was his. He would have eventually made her understand his family, their organization. But not on an exchange. Not with guns in her face. Not when she expected romance and her gave her violence.

"My family…is complicated."

"I think I should just go home, Luca. I don't want anything to do with this."

He leaned against the counter. "You'll have to be more specific, *bella*."

"I don't want complicated."

"What I want from you isn't complicated. And what you need from me isn't complicated." There was nothing complicated in what simmered between them. "Nothing changes between us."

"Everything changes. You're a criminal."

A slow smile spread across his lips. "I'm a businessman who does what it takes to get what he wants." His eyes darkened. "Come here."

She hesitated for a moment. Then she stood and approached him. "I don't want to be a part of whatever this was today."

"You aren't. You're here with me. Kiss me."

"No."

"I didn't ask, Mia. Put your lips against mine, open your mouth, and take my tongue with yours."

Her pulse fluttered in her neck, her eyes slid closed, and she rose onto her tiptoes.

Luca bent his head and waited for her. Her breath warmed his lips. Aroused by the scent of her skin, the touch of her breasts to his chest, and the soft whimper of her surrender, yet he fought the need to pull her flush to him.

Finally, her lips crushed his and her mouth opened. Her fingers curled into his shirt as her tongue licked its way into his mouth.

Luca angled his head and took her mouth in reckless abandon. "You can't tell me you don't want this." His mouth sucked along her neck. "I see your need when you look at me, feel it when you touch me." He gripped her ass, lifted her, and set her on the table in the center of the room.

With his hips between her thighs, he spread her legs. As he claimed her kiss again, he slid his hand to the juncture of her legs, dipped into her panties, and thrust two fingers into her hot, wet, and tight passage.

Mia cried out.

"I'm already in your pussy." He fucked her with his fingers, penetrating but not forcing in too deep, careful to protect her. "Tell me this is mine. That you're mine."

"Yes," she gasped.

"I won't let you go, Mia. I know I come from a fucked up world that is hard to understand. Don't ask me to say more. I don't want to lie to you, but there are things I can't discuss." He slowed his assault on her delicate folds, drawing out the pleasure. His thumb circled her clit.

Her shallow breaths mimicked the play of his fingers.

"Don't come, not yet." He smiled against her lips. "I want my mouth on your pussy, but not until we finish talking."

"Then talk faster," she said. "I want to come."

"Most of my business is with men like Alex. Legitimate business. Look at me. I am the legitimate, legal face of my family. Occasionally, my hands do get dirty. Some of my associates can be dangerous. I promise, I can protect you. Do you trust me?"

"No. But I don't think you trust me either."

She was right. He didn't trust anyone. Not even his brothers. He still wanted her. "We're done talking, Mia."

Luca dropped into the chair, draped her legs over his shoulders, and closed his mouth over her clit. He closed his eyes, taking in her scent, and savoring the hot, almost liquid, softness of her folds.

With a twist of his fingers, she shattered, her silken walls pulsing and creaming.

"Luca," she cried out as she white-knuckle gripped the table. He lapped her juices, empowered that he was the one ruling her body, making her come, and feeling her cunt contract in pleasure.

He slipped his fingers from her body, relished a final taste of her, and lowered her legs. He helped her sit up, and he rested his forehead against hers.

Questions still lingered between them. The haunting shadow in her eyes was a knife wound to the chest. He couldn't leave the questions unanswered. They both held tightly to their secrets, but he couldn't let her believe he didn't hold her safety as his highest priority.

"This isn't the day I had planned for us."

She nodded. "The sailing is nice."

He chuckled. "I wasn't attempting nice. I wanted for us to drive along the cliffs and stop for dinner. And then I wanted you hot and dirty, to bind you to my bed, and discipline your beautiful ass until you screamed my name."

"That would have been nice, too." She combed the hair at his temples with her fingernails. Shivers slithered along his spine, and pressure weighted his balls. The heavy need for release throbbed in his cock, hard from having her taste on his tongue while his fingers had been inside her.

"Nice is a pleasant word. My intentions are far from pleasant. Decadent and perhaps a bit devious."

"Just a bit?"

"I'm afraid I'll never have enough of you. I want to be honest with you, as honest as I can be. But I have to protect my family." He pressed his lips to hers. "I'm offering you my protection."

"I don't need your protection." Her words quivered with fear.

"You'll have it regardless of whether you feel you need it or want it." The Bruno family had enemies.

"No. Here in Italy, out here in the middle of the sea with your business contacts, I understand. But not when we get back to the States."

"We're already here, together. You won't argue with me."

"No, I won't argue." But defiance lit her eyes.

"Don't tempt the lion, Mia. Because I have no intention of letting you go." He crashed his lips against hers, stealing her breath, and leaving no doubt that she was now his.

Chapter Five

Luca held her hand tightly as they walked through the parking garage, the band of his lion ring cutting into her skin. Like the scorching sun in the desert, she could see the anger rising off him in distorted waves. In his other hand, he clutched the black bag.

What was she doing? Luca Bruno was everything she had escaped. Wealth, power, influence…and danger. The Thomas name wasn't associated with organized crime. It should have been.

Now, she was falling, and she didn't know how to stop. Did she want to? Was the threat any more dangerous than when she was in a dungeon with another Dom? With Luca, she didn't need the pain of discipline as much as she needed his demanding commands.

Yet, today, he revealed she'd barely scratched the surface of his control.

The sun was low on the horizon. Outside on the patio, Marco sat with Giada. Savio splashed in the pool. He waved from the water and swam to the edge.

Mia didn't speak as Luca kept her close to his side and spoke to his brother in Italian. He tossed the bag onto the table. Marco's expression remained passive, but a muscle ticked in his jaw.

An arrogant smile twisted Giada's lips as she raked her gaze over Mia.

Mia slipped her fingers from Luca's. "I'll give you a minute."

She crossed the patio to the pool and sat on a deck chair near the water.

Savio smiled and splashed. He rattled off a bunch of words she didn't understand. Assuming he wanted to show her how he could swim, she smiled and nodded. The beautiful dark-haired boy climbed from the pool, turned, and dived in from the edge, splashing her.

She laughed and clapped as he popped back out of the water. Voices behind her grew louder. She couldn't help glancing over her shoulder. Her gaze locked with Luca's. He smiled, and she melted. Butterflies filled her belly.

Giada slid her chair back and crossed to the pool. She spoke to Savio. The little boy wrapped a towel around his shoulders and rushed to his father. Luca ruffled his hair, then Savio ran into the house.

Giada's gaze narrowed on Mia. "Stay away from my son."

She spun and strode toward the house.

Luca had walked away from his brother. As she passed him, she spat several words in Italian. He growled his reply, low and menacing.

Mia didn't need to speak Italian to understand their body language. Nor did she misread his intention as he stalked closer to her. When he was a few steps from her, she stood.

Luca wrapped his fingers around the back of her neck and pulled her hard against his body. His mouth covered hers, his tongue thrusting past her lips.

She whimpered, her arms hanging at her sides, and surrendered. His hand tightened in her hair, forcing her head back as he kissed along her jaw. He pulled back only enough to stare hard into her eyes. "Are you ready to go to bed?"

Fiery lust burned through her. "I am."

He banded an arm around her waist, his large hand holding her hip, and walked toward the table. He spoke to his brother. Marco nodded once.

Luca released a breath, his palm gripping her hip.

"Is everything okay?" she asked as they entered the house.

"We're Italian. We fight—and love with passion. We didn't agree today. But I take orders from Marco."

"About today?"

He nodded. They passed the bedroom door and continued down the hall. "My orders were to go alone. My choice was to bring you with me."

"So, you defied your brother?"

He stopped at a closed door. "And I will defy him again when it comes to you." He cupped her cheek. "This is my dungeon. Take off your clothes."

She glanced down the corridor. They were alone. She slid the zipper, the sound a whir in the quiet space. The fabric slipped down her body and pooled at her feet. Shivers rippled over her flesh. Because of the cut of the dress, she hadn't worn a bra.

Mia stood before him in panties and heels. With the slightest nod of his head, she responded. Snagging her panties with her thumbs, she slid them over her hips, bent over, and removed them. She dropped them onto the dress. With her hand braced on the wall, she removed her shoes, leaving them on the floor.

Luca turned the handle, opened the door, and flipped on the light.

His dungeon. Her gaze swept the room, from the St. Andrew's Cross to the suspension racks, stocks, and a cage. Unlike Protocol with steel and chrome, the room was warm and rustic. The dark stone tile shimmered under the amber-tinted light from lion head sconces on the walls.

All the bondage and punishment furniture had been crafted from polished wood. Two leather chairs banked a stone fireplace in the corner. Floggers, whips, rope, and chain hung from leather boards on the walls. A sex swing hung from thick chains anchored to the ceiling.

And the four-post bed. Square four-by-four beams rose to the ceiling at the corners and also created the canopy. Her heart pounded, the first cracks in her resolve showing. With him, she wasn't Tinker anymore. She hardly remembered what it meant to be property of the dungeon.

In all the time, she'd held to the belief that, when perfectly played, she'd be able to walk away from her life and exist simply for the man she could serve. All she wanted was not to be Mia — the woman Luca would command her to be.

"Here, you will be my Tinker."

She shivered at the darkly whispered name. He'd almost made her forget why he wanted her, what he wanted from her. "Tonight, I'm yours."

"We both know this goes beyond tonight." He chuckled. The dark and dangerous sound seeped under her skin. "You're my submissive. I expect your obedience. There will be no more secrets between us."

Like the warming of a frozen lake, the cracks grew louder, a roar of danger in her ears. No secrets. There were always secrets.

"*Bellissima.*" He bent his head and sipped her lips with a slow drugging kiss. Gentle suction teased her upper lip as she tasted his lower. The velvet heat of his tongue curled around hers. He groaned and kissed her deeper, tasting, seducing her with nothing more than his masterful mouth.

"Do you remember your safeword?"

"*Rossa.*"

"Good girl."

Luca stripped out of his shirt as he crossed to the chest of drawers. Scorching heat and anticipation hummed through her veins. The scent of leather and spice surrounded her. This room was Luca. Dark, intense, a promise of delicious torment.

Mia couldn't slow her responses. An invisible string from her nipples to her clit thrummed with desire. Cream slicked her folds, tinting the air with the scent of her arousal.

"Stand at the end of the bed." He tossed wrist and ankle cuffs to the mattress. Small clamps jangled in his palm.

She instinctively responded to his command.

He took her hand in his, rubbing his fingertip over her knuckles. "I will deny you nothing." He brought her fingers to his lips. "I know what you need, the discipline, the pain—" He moved her hand to his chest. "But I won't take your innocence."

She swallowed. In that moment, she realized she no longer needed it. Her heart pounded so hard she felt as if her ribs were the only thing holding it within her chest. "Luca?"

He rested his forehead against hers. "When you're ready, I'm here."

She nodded.

"But we will still have our play. Remember, *rossa*, because you will be screaming my name tonight."

"Yes, Sir." Lust built within her as he buckled the cuffs to her wrists.

"I can see you thinking," he said as he bent then covered her nipple with his mouth, sucking hard and sinking his teeth into her flesh.

The unexpected intensity took her breath. She gripped his head, curling her fingers into his hair, and pressed into his mouth. His chuckle sent vibrations through her. "I can't think with you touching me."

But she was thinking, wondering how she could endure the pleasure of his man and not fall under his command for more. Because in the end, her submission wouldn't be enough…for either of them. And she was too afraid to let him in.

But they had tonight.

She mourned the loss of his mouth but rejoiced in the pain streaking through her nipple as he tightened the screw clamp to the tip.

So tight. She sucked in a breath, holding it until the pain softened into a throbbing warmth. Then his mouth was on her again. She tensed waiting for the pain and then crying out as he tortured her nipple into a tight bud and screwing down the clamp.

"I only have to touch you here to know if you enjoy the pain." He cupped her pussy in his palm, sliding his finger between her drenched folds, and into her weeping center.

He brought his fingers to his mouth and sucked her juices. "I dream about your pussy, *bella*. So sweet." He kissed her. "Turn around."

Luca trailed kisses along her arm. The touch tickled just enough to make her smile. With a measure of chain, he connected the D-ring on her wrist cuff to the heavy steel O-ring in the center of the left side four-by-four post. Once he had both arms stretched wide and secured to the bed, he spread her legs and chained her ankles to the floor.

"I want you to remember tonight, *amore mio*." He lifted a strand whip from the wall.

Mia swallowed hard, longing for the pain he was about to rain over her body. Unlike a leather whip, the rubber tassels would sting like fire. She ached for the blistering passion.

The first slaps of the falls warmed the flesh of her buttocks. A contented sigh slipped from her lips as she absorbed the stinging lashes. The intensity quickly escalated. A flurry of Italian words spewed from Luca. She wasn't sure from gratification or anger. It didn't matter. He burned thoughts from her mind with the fiery heat of the whip.

She screamed as the lashes morphed into excruciating bites. Her body trembled, her pussy throbbed, and her mind floated in an intoxicating mix of pain and pleasure.

Cream dripped onto her thighs. The tails of the whip slapped her wet skin with searing stings.

Then the lashes ceased. Her heart pounded and the tension eased from her body. A gasp softened into an aching moan. Her gasp. Her desperate need for more. Pleasure streaked from nipple to clit as dark desires burned through her.

Luca's sweat-slicked chest pressed against her back. His lips brushed her shoulder as he reached around her torso. One hand splayed over her belly, grinding her hot, tender flesh into the rough fabric of his jeans. His other hand touched her nipple, letting the screw loose. Pain, like a million sharp needles, ripped through the tip. The hand on her belly slid between her thighs and homed in on her swollen clit.

"Come on my fingers, Mia."

She wailed as violent shudders racked her body. Pain sliced through her breasts and euphoric bliss centered on her pussy. He sucked her neck, biting, and marking her.

Before she could catch her breath, he removed the other clamp, then pinched her nipple in agonizing pressure. Her body jolted. She cried his name as his fingers moved inside of her, deeper than he'd ever been but not enough. She wanted more.

He released her arms from the chains. She draped forward, her chest against the bed. He held her with a palm to her back, his other tenderly caressing her buttocks. She pushed against his hand, wanting his fingers inside her again.

Abandoned by his touch, she tensed with the sound of a metal buckle unhooking, the slide of leather against denim, and the whir of a zipper. She glanced over her shoulder. The fly of his jeans gaped, the head of his cock peaking over the edge of his boxers. Pre-cum seeped from the slit, glistening on the head making her salivate.

"Do you have something to say?"

Mia licked her lips and shook her head.

"Yes, I think you do." Luca chuckled, dropped to his knees, and licked her pussy with the softest touch of his tongue. She whimpered. The sweet torture was harder to bear than the bite of the belt she expected. Uncontrollable quivering overtook her legs. His fingers dug into her as he spread her ass cheeks. His tongue and lips played against her, tasting, licking, and nibbling her from slit to rosette.

"Oh god," she muffled into the bedding, biting the blanket as another orgasm washed over her. He wrecked her, driving her past pleasure, careening head-on into crazy.

Just as she was able to catch her breath, the crack of the belt cut the silence. She moaned, drowning again in the blurred waters of pain and pleasure. Her back arched, and her ass rose to meet the blistering heat. He fed her addiction, sating the gnawing craving for more. Her eyes closed as tears slipped onto her cheeks, trailed along her face, and soaked into the bedding.

Floating on a wave of emotions, her body responded, sliding into another release. "Luca," the word was barely a whisper. And then he was there, lifting her into his arms, cradling her against his chest, speaking tender words in Italian.

"*Mia dolce sottomessa*. My sweet submissive." He carried her through an adjoining door to a giant whirlpool bath. With her on his lap, he filled the tub.

She draped her arms over his shoulders, kissing the smooth yet masculine sun-bronzed flesh of his shoulder. Her fingers curled in the hair at the nape of his neck.

Luca's large, strong hand cascaded along her back, the gold of his ring reminding her who this man was. She'd heard the lion roar.

"I was scared today," she said.

"Look at me."

She stilled, staring into the unyielding depths of his intense eyes. Butterflies flitted in her belly. She was here because she hated…and loved everything about him.

"You don't have to fear me. I know it's hard to trust. But I promise, this—my family, work, this fucked up life—will never touch you."

The conviction in his voice worked to persuade her, but he couldn't keep that promise. No one could. Still, her heart ached with the want to believe.

He slipped the tie from her hair. With deliberate slowness, he loosened the braid, his fingers combing through the wind-blown tangles. His gaze roamed over her face, a hint of a grin tugging on his lips. "I'd never let anyone hurt you."

She drew in a shallow breath, fighting her addiction. She wanted to feel his touch. No one else had commanded her submission, understood her needs.

She would never be safe, not as long as she craved Luca.

He helped her into the warm water. "Take care with your beautiful ass."

"Aren't you going to get in?" She hissed with the delicious sting from her welts and redness.

"I thought you may want to soak." He paused at the door.

"I don't want to be alone," she confessed.

He pushed his jeans and boxers down his legs, stepped out of them, revealing his beautiful, hard cock. Veins, thick and pulsing, roped the length.

"Sir." A torrent of need swirled within her. "*Please.*" She hoped the one word would reveal her feelings and need for him.

Luca cradled her head in his large palm. She opened her mouth, and he slid his cock between her lips.

Harshly spoken Italian words tumbled from his lips. His jaw clenched, but his intense focus was on her face, her mouth, as she stretched her lips and swallowed more of his cock. Hot smooth skin rubbed against her tongue, the salty essence making her mouth water.

Mia ran her fingers along the back of his thighs, taking him deeper into her mouth. She swallowed around the thickness, pillowing the head against her tongue. With a moan, she pulled her lips along the length, letting her teeth barely graze the sensitive, velvety flesh.

With a roar, he ejaculated. Hot cream streamed into her throat. She swallowed as she squeezed her hand, pumping his shaft hard through his orgasm. He gasped for breath. Abdominals quivered and muscles in his thighs bunched and tensed beneath her fingers. And she continued to suck, lick, and pleasure his cock with her mouth.

His fingers loosened in her hair, his touch gentling. A shuddering exhale vibrated through him as his cock eased from between her lips. She smiled as he slipped into the water with her.

Leaning back against the curved tub, he pulled Mia into his arms, her back flush against his chest.

She sighed, letting him absorb her weight. "I wish we could stay like this forever."

His lips brushed her temple. "You'll turn into a prune."

Water sloshed in the tub as she turned and glanced over her shoulder. "Soft, wrinkly, and sweet?"

He kissed her. "Definitely soft and sweet."

She settled back against his chest. His fingers trailed over her belly, covered her breasts, and rasped over her beaded nipples. The warm water relaxed him, seemingly to be content with the silence and the feel of her in his arms.

"Are you asleep?" she asked with a little giggle. He'd grown so silent and still. She turned in his arms.

"Almost." Luca shifted and stood. After stepping from the bath, he held a fluffy white towel open for her. Never taking his gaze from hers, he blotted the rivulets of water from her face. With a tender touch, he dried her body. Then he quickly dried himself.

"Do you want to sleep here or return to my bed?"

"Here." Even at home, she preferred to sleep in the dungeon. Contentment washed over her as she climbed onto the bed. Once Luca was next to her, she cuddled into his warmth. He'd slept naked next to her night after night and hadn't plied his incredible prowess against her or attempted to seduce her into giving him her virginity.

He sighed, his breathing became even and steady, and his body grew lax against her. Her heart ached for him and the responsibility he carried for his family. Those pressures had killed Oliver. Organized crime had killed her parents. And she'd fallen in love with a Mafioso.

She did love him. Pain, the pain she chased with BDSM, the pain that robbed her of breath and shattered her security, cut deep into her chest, carving out a hole deep enough to bury what was left of her soul.

She thought of the life she cherished at Protocol, knowing she would leave it all behind to stay with Luca. But there were some things she couldn't escape. And some truths she couldn't deny. His life would eventually kill him, too, and if she gave herself to him, she wouldn't survive without him.

Mia pressed her lips to his chest. He stirred in his sleep. She flicked her tongue against his nipple, gently nipping his skin.

Pushing the sheet and blanket down to the bottom of the bed, she exposed his beautifully honed body. Dark hair dusted his pectorals, feathered along his grooved abdominals, and trailed to the thatch of dark, springy hair surrounding his hardening dick.

She closed her lips over the crown. Luca palmed her head, tunneling his fingers into her hair.

Sliding her leg over his lap, she straddled his groin, sliding her pussy along his shaft. Moisture flooded her core, and a piercing ache clenched her heart. She braced her hands on his chest and rocked against him.

Fear gripped her. Fear of giving in, fear of how he'd changed her, and fear of losing who she'd always wanted to be. And knowing whatever she did, her heart would be crushed.

Firm hands gripped her hips. Her gaze locked with his darkening eyes.

"Mia?" He held perfectly still.

Tears slipped onto her cheeks. She lifted onto her knees, and with her fingers around his shaft, slid the head through her wet folds. And then she slowly lowered.

Searing pain stretched her opening. She lifted and whimpered as she attempted to take another inch. His cock was too big or her passage too small. She gritted her teeth, but there was no pleasure, just tearing pain.

"Slow," he whispered.

"Help me."

He reached between her legs and slid his finger along her clit. Tiny sparks of pleasure burst inside of her.

"Lift up." She obeyed, and he curled two fingers into her passage. Cream slicked his hand. A third finger stretched her wider. He pumped into her, scissoring, grinding, and opening her passage. Then he moved his fingers to her clit again.

This time when she sank onto his shaft, her walls quivered, softened and she sank onto his length. She cried out as she was fully impaled on his cock.

Luca growled, his neck stretching as he thrust inside of her. Gripping her hips hard, he anchored her to his lap. He filled her, the burning intrusion morphing into a desperate need to move against him.

"Don't move, *bella*." He sat, wrapping his arms around her. Her legs shifted to circle around his back. He kissed her lips, nuzzled her neck, and then pivoted, pinning her back to the bed.

He slowly withdrew from her body. With a soft moan, he slid back into her heated core, continuing the steady rhythm, angling her pelvis to take more of his cock.

Pleasure blurred with the simmering pain. She gripped his shoulders, her back arching.

"Oh my god," she said on a breath.

Luca stared into her eyes as he continued the tormenting control of thrust and retreat. She'd never felt so complete and connected. Where he ended, she began. He rocked into her body in a wicked dance, a building crescendo. Flutters rippled inside her. Blinding light built behind her eyes.

"Luca," she cried as a wave of pleasure she'd never felt before washed over her. She gasped for breath, her entire body convulsing, and her passage constricting against the fullness of Luca's cock.

Her orgasm spurred him into a punishing intensity. He thrust into her, fucking her into the mattress until he roared her name. Hot cum slicked her inner walls as he continued to fill her with thrust after thrust.

Mia held tight to his shoulders, drowning in the swirling storm of his release. After several deep breaths, he collapsed onto her. Trembles surged through her as she absorbed the weight of his body. She kept her legs locked around his hips, unwilling to lose the connection where he joined with her.

He hugged her tightly and buried his face in her neck. With tenderness, he kissed her, a slow seductive kiss full of erotic heat and desperate passion. His tongue searched for hers, tangling and tasting.

Finally, he slipped from her body. Rolling to his side, he kept her tucked against his chest.

"Does this mean your mine?"

Her heart pounded in her chest. She wanted to tell him yes because she would always belong to him. But those weren't the words.

"No," she whispered. "This means I love you."

His grip tightened on her. She closed her eyes, knowing she'd never be Tinker again. But she wasn't sure she'd ever be ready to be Mia.

Chapter Six

A knock sounded at the door. Before Luca could reply, Carlo stepped into the room. He held Mia's clothes and shoes in his hand.

"These were in the hall." His gaze narrowed on Mia. "What the fuck did you do to her? You fucking hurt her?" His Italian came in hard bursts. "Does she need a doctor? Luca, you went too far. Fuck."

Luca blinked sleep from his eyes and leaned up on his elbows. Mia was draped across his chest. A rose blush bloomed across her flesh and welts crisscrossed her buttocks and thighs. But it was the stain of red between her legs and down her thighs that had Carlo's attention.

Luca covered her with the sheet. "She's fine."

Carlo's hands curled into fists. "She doesn't look fine."

"*Innocente*," he said. "I was her first."

"Luca, no." Carlo raked his fingers through his hair. "She's okay?"

"She's mine."

As if to prove his assurance, she yawned and stretched, the sheet molding to the roundness of her ass.

"Yes, now get your eyes off her. Tell me why you're in my dungeon at three in the morning and then leave us." He ran his hands under the sheet, cupping her ass.

"No time. Marco is on his way. We got problems. Greco's a rat. Gonna get burned and you need to be out of the country. Marco wants you to do the delivery of the diamonds."

"Fucking Marco." Apparently, he was still pissed that Luca had involved Mia in the pickup. "Fuck me." If he had to make the delivery, his life was about to get complicated. "Twenty minutes."

"You'll be lucky to get ten."

Let the plane leave without him. He nodded to Carlo. "Ten. Get someone to pack our bags."

Carlo left the room, and Luca slid out from Mia.

She yawned and stretched again. "More sleep."

"I'm afraid this was our last night. Business requires me to return to the States."

"Today?"

"Now." He nuzzled her neck. "Carlo is seeing to our things. Get dressed."

She pushed the sheets off and stared at the reminder of last night staining her thighs. "Can we shower?"

Marco could wait. He wanted inside her again. Now. His cock hardened as he took her hand. "We'll need to hurry."

"I guess that is on you. To come, all I need is you touching me and your permission."

***

Heat simmered in Luca's gut. Part of him was glad to get back to the States, away from Italy where he would have Mia alone. However, he wouldn't allow his annoyance with Marco and Giada, or his desire for Mia to undermine his responsibilities to the family.

"Your ten minutes and mine are vastly different," Carlo said in Italian as he approached Luca in the hall.

Mia walked next to Luca, elegant in a calf-length halter dress with a wide belt. Carlo smiled.

"You have excellent taste in clothes," she said to him. "Thank you for choosing such lovely things for me."

"Because I told him to," Luca grumbled.

"Are you jealous?" She linked her arm with his.

Not usually. But he wanted her back in his dungeon, locked away from anyone looking at her or touching her.

Carlo laughed. "I suppose she's worth Marco's wrath."

Luca gaze lingered on her soft blonde hair falling past her shoulders, the feminine slope of her spine, and the sway of her breasts. Yes, she was worth it.

Marco paced in the kitchen. The house was eerily quiet.

"Get on the fucking plane, Luca." There was no buildup to pissed. Marco's furious words, spoken in Italian, ricocheted off the walls. "You risk our business for a piece of ass. Is American pussy so good you fuck over your responsibilities, you piece of shit? What the fuck is wrong with you? We have traitors inside the organization. Do you even know who she is?"

"She's mine," he said and turned to Carlo. "Take her to the plane. I need a few words with my brother, and then I need to kiss Savio goodbye."

Luca waited until Carlo escorted her from the room.

"You need to put your dick away and think with your head." Marco seethed with pent up anger. His hardened jaw clenched. He rolled his shoulders. "You have ten million dollars in raw diamonds and another fifteen in cut to deliver and you're more concerned with that shit you do in your torture chamber."

"This is your fucking disaster, Marco. Not mine. My hands are clean. You need to see they stay that way. Sending the diamonds with me is some fucked up power play with you. I don't want your place in the family. You need me right where I am. Squeaky fucking clean."

"You're a Bruno. None of us are fucking clean."

Luca strode down the hall to Giada and Savio's wing of the estate.

Marco continued to holler. "Savio is asleep. He's with his nanny. Go now, Luca. He won't even notice you've gone."

"He's *my* son, Marco." Regardless of parentage, he'd claimed him the moment Giada found out she was pregnant. He didn't care who Giada had been fucking. Savio was a Bruno. That was all that mattered.

***

Luca boarded the plane. His words with Marco still burned in his gut.

Mia sat in the corner of the couch with her hands in her lap. Carlo sat next to her, his giant frame eating up most of the space.

"You're going to upgrade the bitch back to cunt," Carlo said in Italian. The only woman Carlo called a cunt was Giada.

"Where is she?"

Carlo nodded to the bedroom. "She needs reminded that her mouth is best used for sucking Bruno cock and not speaking to your woman."

Luca took Mia's hand and dragged her toward the rear of the plane.

"Luca, no." She tried to pull away. "I'm not going to cause a scene with your ex. She's the mother of your son. Please don't put me in the middle of whatever this is between the two of you."

"There hasn't been anything between us since before Savio was born." Before then, he'd been a fool to think she was anything more than a beautiful face. "How can I make you understand?"

How to explain Giada's position in his family.

"Tinker, Giada is a cunt," Carlo said. "She's using you to get under Luca's skin. This isn't your fight."

"Thank you," Luca said sarcastically. "But I don't need your help."

"I'm not going in there." She sat on the couch again.

Carlo laughed as Luca strode to the bedroom door and opened it. He spoke to Giada in Italian. "What did you say to her?"

Giada braced a hand on her hip. "Only what she needed to hear." She sauntered closer to him. "We're going to spend the next few days together. The buyer expects a hot Italian couple that can't keep their hands off each other." She leaned in bringing her lips close to his ear. "Maybe we should practice."

"The buyer expects diamonds. You make the exchange. I make sure they know who they are dealing with. You usually do this business with Stefano. Are you fucking him, too? Are there any Bruno men left you haven't fucked?"

"Insurance."

"Your pussy ensures your position in the family. Not because you're fucking a Bruno but because you'll fuck anyone for Marco."

"And if he wants me to fuck you?"

"You want in my dungeon, Giada? I'd love to put a gag in your mouth." He peeled her hand off his chest. "I'm sure we all would appreciate a minute of quiet."

"Get a drink, Luca," she said. "It's going to be a long flight."

And an even longer week. He followed Giada back into the main cabin of the plane. He sat next to Mia as the engines roared, the plane raced along the runway, and lifted into the air.

He rested his arm over Mia's thighs. "She's going to glare at you because she hates to see me happy."

Mia smiled. "So, I shouldn't take it personally?"

"No, you should," Giada said from the opposite chair. "I don't know you, and I don't like unknown threats to my family."

"Don't speak to her," Luca said to Giada.

"Don't tell me what to do. I'm not one of your submissive little bitches that obey your rules." Her gaze snapped to Mia. "You didn't think you're his only girlfriend, did you?" She rolled her eyes. "Young and naïve. You're just the newest toy."

Mia averted her gaze, glancing at anything but him. "Come."

He waited for her to comply. After a moment's hesitation, she stood and followed him into the bedroom. Once inside, he closed the door.

"I'm tired," she said.

"Good, then we should rest." He stripped off his shirt and then unbuttoned his jeans.

"We don't need to be undressed to rest, Luca. And I don't need to be the target of Giada's anger."

He paced the room. "Giada is connected to our family in ways that can't be undone. She will always be around." He approached Mia. "More than Savio's mother, she's a member of the family, a made woman. My father will never let her go. She knows this."

"I'm not upset with her. But she does get to you."

"Yes, because her interference has cost me—" He couldn't speak the words. Savio, the relationship with his brother and father— Luca had made the decision they were more important than his need for revenge against Giada. And she hated him for it.

"Marco told me you'll always belong to her."

"She sits out there. You're here." He backed her against the door.

"Is what she said true?"

"Have I played in the dungeon? Yes, the same as you, but you can expect fidelity from me." He kissed along her neck. "I will demand it of you."

She clutched his shoulders as he lifted her dress, bunching it around his arm. He rubbed his finger against the dampness between her legs.

Rather than strip her naked, he tore the crotch of her panties, slammed two fingers into her heat, and ripped a moan from her throat.

She fumbled with the buckle of his belt. "They'll hear us."

"And that excites you."

She couldn't deny it. Her pussy, hot and wet, sucked his fingers.

"Fuck. I need inside you."

"Is this to show her you don't belong to her?"

His jeans dropped, he gripped her ass, crashed her against the door, and thrust his cock into her slick entrance. "No, to show you you're mine."

Mia cried out, her legs tightened around his hips, and her shoes slipped from her feet. He grunted, slamming in and out of her tight cunt squeezing his dick in exquisite pressure. The door creaked and groaned as he fucked her hard and fast. Her smooth inner tissue gloved him in ecstasy.

With one arm around his shoulders and the other smacking the door hard, she thrust against him.

He dug his fingers into her ass, gripping her as he pounded into her until his balls pressed between them.

"Let me hear you." He bit down hard on her shoulder.

She moaned as she pulsed and contracted with her orgasm. The pressure sent him over the edge. He continued to thrust into her, a slippery slide into oblivion on their mingling cream.

Luca kissed her lips as he carried her to the bed. He set her on her feet. As he stared into her eyes, he pulled the tie of her halter dress. The fabric slipped to the floor. He tugged her torn panties down her thighs, still wet with his cum.

He yanked off his T-shirt and wiped her legs with the soft cotton.

Once he stripped, he pulled back the bedspread. She climbed between the sheets, and he spooned in behind her. "We need to talk."

"I know."

"You were a virgin. There was no worry for me. But I should've stopped us, protected you."

"I didn't think about a condom. I just wanted you inside of me."

"And now that is the only place I want to be. I've never had sex without a condom until you."

She stiffened in his arms. "What about Savio? At least once without protection."

He lifted onto one arm. "Never without a condom. Only you."

She swallowed. "What are you telling me?"

Something he couldn't put into words. "Only that he is my son." He traced her furrowed brow with his fingertip. "I've been tested. I'm clean. Are we risking pregnancy? Are you on birth control?"

"I'm not. I didn't plan to have sex."

He kissed her forehead. "One day I'll make you a mother, but only if that is what you want. You've said you aren't sure. Either I need to protect you, or you'll need to see a doctor."

She nodded. "I'll take care of it."

He pulled her close again. Silence stretched between them. He wondered if she worried about what could have already occurred between them. She'd only whispered the words once. She loved him.

When she opened her heart, she shared her body and gave him the one thing she held sacred. Yet, something still remained between them. This didn't feel like the beginning of a new relationship. But he couldn't understand why it felt like the end.

***

With the flight time and the time change, Luca had only lost a few hours. The midmorning sun warmed his face as he stood next to the car at the hanger. Giada sat in the front seat. Carlo waited, scanning the area.

"Once Carlo drops us off at the hotel, he'll take you home. I need to make arrangements for my business, but I'll come to you tonight. Perhaps I can spend a few nights in your bed. Or if you prefer, you can stay with me in my suite at the hotel. Giada will be in a separate room."

Tears filled her eyes.

"Don't cry. This business will be over soon."

She rose onto her tiptoes and pressed her lips to his. "I'll be fine. Just remember, I love you."

He sealed his lips to hers, sliding his tongue into her mouth. She clung to him, desperation in her kiss. Her arm brushed the gun strapped to his waist, and she tensed.

Luca broke the kiss. "You understand why it's necessary."

She nodded.

"And you know that family business isn't discussed. I don't want you to see Alex or go to High Protocol unless you're with me. I've shared my family with you."

"Don't worry. I'm not a threat to you."

"Fuck, don't you think I know that." He pulled her close again.

"We need to go," Carlo said.

Luca opened the door for her. She slid into the back seat, and he followed her. He held her trembling hand, rubbing his thumb over her knuckles. Until he made the exchange with Giada, he couldn't risk Mia's safety.

They pulled up to the hotel. Carlo walked around the front of the vehicle and opened the door for Giada. As soon as Giada was out of the car, Luca kissed Mia. He didn't want to leave her, didn't want this tension between them, but he had responsibilities.

There wasn't anything left to say. Sweat trickled along his spine, and his heart pounded. He curved his fingers around her neck, hovered his lips over hers, and inhaled her breath.

"*Ti amo.*" He loved her. Needing to show her, he kissed her hard, briefly sweeping her mouth with his tongue, and then he slid from the car.

Luca leaned in and spoke to his consigliere. "Take care of her. Protect her."

Carlo nodded and slid back behind the wheel. "With my life."

***

Mia watched out the back window as Luca walked next to Giada into the hotel. Her heart ached, and her tummy roiled.

"Where to?" Carlo asked from the front seat.

A touch of fear tightened her throat. Would Carlo do as she asked, or would he call Luca?

"High Protocol." She met Carlo's gaze in the rearview mirror. She smiled, hoping he didn't question her motives. "I need my phone, my ID, my keys. I left everything when Luca whisked me away."

"No problem."

She settled into the seat until they reached the club. "Thank you. There's no need for you to wait." She wanted him to leave, wanted to be able to put distance between her and Luca. "I can get home from here."

"Luca insisted."

"It'll be a few minutes." She tried to walk casually to the club doors. Pressing the buzzer, she waited for someone to let her in. Deliveries were made during the day so either Chris or Ronan would be around.

The door popped open.

"What the fuck, Tinker?" Ronan pulled her into the club and wrapped his arms around her. He kissed her temple and held her. "Where the fuck have you been?"

She couldn't stop the tears from falling. She clung to Ronan and sobbed.

"Ah, Tink. I'm sorry," Ronan whispered into her hair, quietly trying to calm her. "It's okay. You scared the fuck out of us." He inched her back and tipped her face to his. "What happened?"

She shook her head.

"Do I need to beat the shit out of someone?"

"No." The Doms in the club wouldn't be a match for Luca and Carlo…or their associates. Bringing the Mafia into Protocol was the last thing she intended to do. "I'm not in trouble, Ronan. You don't need to worry."

"I'm always going to worry." He pulled her into his arms again. "You've never lied to me before."

She mentally groaned. Maybe not about a scene. But she'd never been truthful with anyone in the club.

"When you're ready?" He kissed her head.

"I just stopped to get my phone and stuff. It's behind the bar."

"Whatever you need. You know I'm here for you. You should talk to the Professor. He's worried. Fuck, Tink. I've never seen him so upset."

"I know. I will, but I need a couple days." She needed to figure out what she did now. Because stepping into the club, she accepted that she couldn't go back to being Tinker.

Her phone had a single bar. She only needed enough power for one phone call.

"Where the fuck are you?" Hudson asked.

She expected his anger. "Protocol. Pick me up but come to the private entrance in the garage."

"Fifteen minutes."

Her phone died. And so did the rest of her heart.

Avoiding Ronan in the club, she made her way to the private garage. Standing in the shadow of a cement pylon, she waited. Fear snaked through her mind every time a car drove near.

With Carlo out front waiting for her, she didn't worry about Luca. But if Alex or the Professor showed up, they wouldn't be as easily dissuaded. Alex would question her time with Luca, and the Professor would take one look at her and know she was no longer his Tinker.

A familiar black sedan pulled around the corner. She stepped from the shadow, opened the back door, and climbed into the car.

Hudson's mouth hardened as he pulled out of the garage. She couldn't stop the last glance at Carlo smoking a cigarette outside the club. He stared at the door, then checked his watch. How long would it take for him to realize she wasn't coming out?

"Where were you?"

"With a friend." She stared out the window.

"Do I need to see what he did to you to know what kind of friend?" His knuckles whitened as he gripped the steering wheel.

"Don't chastise me. I know you're upset. And you have every right to be. But I'm an adult. I don't need permission."

"Don't fucking talk about permission, Mia. You live for their permission. The Doms in that club get off on controlling every part of you. Forgive me if I want to know where you are and that you're not hurt. I'm scared for you—and for me. I love you, sweetheart. Someday, one of them is going to go too far."

Tears rolled down her cheeks. "It doesn't matter now. I'm not going back."

Not to Luca…maybe not to Protocol. Falling in love had fucked up her life.

The thought of being with another Dom in the club turned her stomach. But she couldn't live with Luca. She wouldn't live with another loss of someone she loved.

"Just take me home." Where she could go to her dungeon and suffer alone with her misery.

Once they were through the gate and headed to the house, Mia released the breath she'd been holding. She was safe behind the fences. No one knew who she was or where to find her. As long as she stayed out of Protocol, not even Alex would know where to look.

Hudson parked in front of the house. Without waiting for him to get the door, she climbed from the car. She took two steps, and she was in his arms. He held her tightly.

"Don't scare me like this. I can't fucking take it," he said. "I don't care what shit you're into, you won't go radio silent on me again." He pulled back and stared into her eyes. "Get me, Mia. You're not out of my sight."

She nodded as Poppy came bustling out of the house.

"I'm sorry," she said. Not about Luca, but for not realizing how she'd made them worry.

"Are you hungry?"

She smiled at Poppy. "I am." She wasn't sure she could eat, but she didn't want to be alone. "Don't leave," she said to Hudson.

He wrapped his arm around her. "Fuck. About time you realize you need me."

"I do."

***

Luca paced across the hotel suite. Giada sat on the couch with a glass of wine and a smirk on her lips.

"Where the fuck is she?"

"I don't know. She wanted to stop at the club for her phone. Asked me to wait. I did. Fucking forty-five minutes later, I went to the door. Asked the guy there where she was. He didn't know, but I got his name. Ronan. He looked. She was gone."

Luca raked his hands through his hair. Panic roared through him. "Why would she leave without saying anything to you?"

"Maybe you don't know her at all," Giada said as she inspected her nail polish. "I think I'll go to the hotel salon."

"Go." Luca waved her off. "Don't leave the hotel." He turned to Carlo. "Get the car. We're going to the club."

He had no other way of finding Mia. No phone number, no address, nothing. At least, he knew her name. Otherwise, he'd be tearing apart the city, looking for a submissive named Tinker.

They drove to the club, buzzed the door, and asked to see Alex.

The security guard glanced to Carlo. "Can't let you in the club."

Carlo had a gun strapped to his chest. He buttoned his jacket.

Somehow, the security guard alerted his team of a potential situation. Several large bouncers appeared, one at the door to the dungeon, two at the doorway to the club offices. Luca groaned and rolled his shoulders. The distinct click of a gun sounded from the goon at the door.

"Carlo is my bodyguard. He carries a weapon for my safety, which is why he has never been in the club with me prior to tonight." He nodded to Carlo. "I just need to talk to Alex about Tinker. Wait outside."

"She's not here," the head of security said just as Ronan burst through the door.

"What the fuck is going on?" His gaze snapped to Luca.

"I need to speak with Tinker," Luca said.

Ronan dismissed security. "I haven't seen her since this afternoon. She was upset, didn't want to talk about it, so perhaps you and I should talk. I have a few questions for you."

Luca followed him through the door to his office.

"What happened, Luca?"

"I don't know," he said. "I took her home with me, to Italy, for my son's birthday." He released a sigh of frustration. "After the time we spent together, what happened between us, why would she run?"

"What the fuck did you do?" Ronan came around the desk. "Did you break her?"

"Fuck, Ronan. No! I didn't break her," he said. "I just need to talk to her. Give me her phone number."

"I can't. Membership records are confidential."

"Call Ferraro," Luca demanded. "Get permission."

"I'm telling you he won't give it." But Ronan picked up his phone and made the call anyway. "Boss, we have a problem. It's Tinker."

Luca paced as Ronan spoke on the phone. They would take too long. He dialed Carlo on his phone. As soon as he answered, he spoke in Italian. "Find her. Mia Toliver. Just find her."

He disconnected and turned to Ronan.

"Alex is on his way. He won't give you her information, but he said he'll contact you."

Ronan closed the space between them. "We made it clear. Tinker belongs to the club."

"Not anymore." He stepped toward the door. "Once I find her, she'll tell you where she belongs."

"We better find her, or your—"

Luca didn't wait for the rest of the threat. He stormed from the office. Right now, he needed their help. He needed to find Mia. No way did she just walk away. Something was wrong.

A sick feeling coiled in his gut. He approached Carlo. "This better not be the work of Marco or Giada."

"You really think they'd touch the girl?" Carlo asked as they walked to the car.

"I think they would if they believed she'd get in their way. They want to keep me in line."

Carlo put his hand on Luca's bicep, slowing their progression. "You know my loyalty is to you, not the family."

Luca nodded. "I know. Same."

They climbed back into the car. "Where to?"

Luca didn't have a clue. "Back to the hotel."

If she was in trouble, she'd know where to find him.

Chapter Seven

Last night, Luca hadn't sleep. Carlo had his contacts digging for any information on Mia Toliver, but the woman was a ghost. No public records, no footprint in social media, not a fucking crumb. The name didn't exist. Who the fuck had he fallen in love with?

Unlike Carlo, he didn't believe for a moment she was connected to any of his enemies. She was known as Tinker in the club, and she'd been there long before him. Their meeting wasn't planned, and she wasn't part of any syndicate.

After room service had brought up coffee and breakfast, he'd sent Alex a text but hadn't heard back.

"We have a meeting tonight, first for drinks, followed by dinner." Giada rested her hand on her hip. "You need to get your shit together." She crossed to the bar and poured a glass of wine. "All this drama for a piece of ass."

Luca stormed across the room and, in a flash, pinned her against the wall. His forearm pressed against her collarbone. "Did you do this?"

"Stop," she gasped, her nails clawing his skin.

"If you and Marco had anything to do with her disappearance, I'll fucking kill you."

"Luca!" Carlo yelled.

Luca shoved away from her.

"What the fuck is wrong with you?" she screamed. "This deal has been planned for months. None of us knew about her. When could we have set her up? Figure your shit out, Luca. You're making mistakes. Mistakes get people killed." She rubbed her neck. "If I wanted your bitch out of the picture, she'd be dead."

Luca's cell rang. He rushed to the phone. "Alex. Is she okay?"

"There's a problem." Alex's voice was dark and somber.

Luca sat on a chair. "Where is she?"

"Not only do I not know where she is, I don't know who she is."

"What? You know her."

Alex all but claimed her as his. How could he not know her? But then Luca had told her he loved her, and he didn't have a fucking clue who she was or how to reach her.

"I know a woman named Tinker."

Only in the club. "Her name is Mia Toliver."

Alex was quiet a moment. "Her membership to High Protocol lists her name as Iris White. My business partner is connected. He's doing a deep dive, but he's come up empty so far. I'll have him add Mia Toliver to the search."

Luca ran his hand over his head. "I don't understand. Why would she do this?"

Alex sighed. "I don't know, my friend. For the last three years, she's been in my club every night. She's a sweet girl, but she was always quiet about her personal life."

And no one cared to look any deeper.

"Did you know both of her parents are dead, and so is her brother. Not sure if that will help."

"Any other details?"

"Her brother committed suicide. She was a twin." Part of him hated sharing her secrets, but the bigger part of him just wanted to find her and make sure she wasn't injured, hadn't fallen victim to Giada or Marco—or any enemy of the Bruno family. Not knowing was ripping him apart.

A defeated sigh crossed the line. "I want to find her as badly as you do, Luca."

Pressure burned behind his eyes. "I doubt that, but I appreciate the help."

He disconnected from Alex wondering what to do next and tapped the phone against his chin. He closed his eyes.

Giada sat across from him. "Maybe she doesn't want to be found."

He'd considered that, but then he'd have to believe everything he'd felt with her was a lie.

***

Mia sat across from Poppy and Hudson. They'd given her time to rest, although she hadn't slept much. Not even her pallet in the dungeon had given her the comfort she craved.

But she couldn't think of Luca. Not if she wanted to be strong and figure out what she was going to do with her life. Her time with Luca had given her perspective. She could be strong enough to handle her money, her name, her insecurity…but not her fear. And she couldn't risk a connection to the Mafia.

"I'm going to stop negotiations on all pending sales. I need to rethink what I've been doing." She took a deep breath. "I owe you more than an apology," she said to both of them. "And not just for this last week."

"What happened?" Poppy reached for Mia's hand across the table. "Did those men hurt you?"

Mia shook her head. "Not this one." She blinked tears from her eyes. "But he wouldn't be good for me. He lives a dangerous life. I can't love someone whose work is going to get him killed." Her gaze shifted to Hudson. "I know you understand."

He'd been in Special Forces and lost too many brothers in too many wars.

"But he's not really the issue. His family is. And I would be too much temptation for them," she continued. "He's part of the Bruno family. A Mafioso. And they deal in diamonds."

Hudson cursed. "Christ, Mia."

"I know. But he doesn't know who I am. He met Tinker." She curled her fingers around the warmth of her coffee cup. "I fell hard. I love him, but his brother is dangerous."

"I'm going to need names and locations of where you were."

"Luca Bruno. But he's not dangerous. At least, not the way his brother Marco is. Luca has legitimate business here. That's how I met him."

"Where did you meet him?"

"Protocol. He's doing business with Alex Ferraro." She narrowed her gaze on Hudson. "Don't dig into Alex's business. Don't involve anyone at all. I just want you to make sure nothing comes back to me—or to either of you." She'd brought dangerous men to their doorstep. She pushed away from the table. "As long as we don't have any connections to the Bruno family, then we don't have to worry. Do we?"

"Maybe. Grant might know more." Hudson refilled his coffee.

"There's more."

Poppy made the sign of the cross.

Mia patted her hand. "Nothing that terrible." Her gaze lifted to Hudson's. "I was with him when he made a pickup. I don't know details because I don't speak Italian."

"Jesus." Hudson pointed his finger at her. "You're not leaving this house again. You involved yourself with the Mafia."

"Not intentionally. And no one saw me, well except Luca and his associates."

"Fuck, I worried because you had a thing for pain. Now, I have to worry about the Mafia putting a hit out on you."

She nodded. "If they find out who I am. Maybe. That's why I want to stop all transactions. I don't want to run the risk of doing business with Luca or any of his associates."

"I want extra guards at the gate."

"Whatever you need to do." She choked back a sob.

He wrapped his arms around her. "Shit. You know how to pick the men in your life. They're either kinky motherfuckers, or they're Mafioso."

"You sound like his consigliere, Carlo." She chuckled as she dried her tears on his shirt. "And Luca is both."

"I need the staff to report anything suspicious. Poppy, no deliveries past the gate until further notice. Mia, you're in my car. Period. You need to be somewhere, I'll take you."

"You can't be with me twenty-four hours a day."

"If the Bruno family is dealing in conflict diamonds out of western Africa, you're in danger. They find out a Thomas is back in the diamond business…"

"I know." Blood diamonds were responsible for much of her wealth…and the death of her parents. Her father had been in bed with the wrong men. Even though the ransom for their return had been paid, both had been executed by guerillas. At least, that was the story she'd been told.

"You can't see him again. He won't have a choice if asked to choose between you and the family."

That was why she ran. "I know Grant is going to want to see me today." She smiled. "Maybe we should leave for a while. I'll buy an island and really disappear."

"Or we untangle this shit, you stop pretending Mia doesn't exist, and you start living life like the powerful heiress I know you are."

"More like a naughty Cinderella. I'm still me. I like being told what to do."

"Good. Go get ready."

She slid from the chair. Time with Luca had changed her. In the dungeon, she'd been searching for a Dom to own her. An arrogant Italian had made her use her safeword before he ever touched her. And then he became everything she never thought she'd want.

Submission and danger didn't have to come with the crack of a whip. She'd become his. She'd need Hudson as a reminder that she was as dangerous to Luca as he was to her.

***

Luca had a gun strapped to his waist and another at his ankle. He had no doubt Carlo was armed with more weapons than a Swiss Army Knife. Giada's dress was a distraction. The tight white dress gloved to every curve on her body. Her dark hair fell around her shoulders. Bright red lips coyly flirted. Diamonds dripped from her ears, and a brilliant pendant rested just above the creamy swell of her breasts. The bitch knew her worth.

Carlo entered the room and cocked a brow at Giada as he crossed to Luca.

"Any word?" Luca asked.

"She doesn't exist. There is an Iris White in New Mexico. Another in LA. Neither are our girl. Same with Mia Toliver. You can find a list of names on social media, but none are Tinker. We won't find her with dead parents and a dead brother and nothing else to go on."

"Am I supposed to just let her go?" Luca asked.

"Or wait for her," Carlo said. "She likes a whip. A girl like her doesn't stay out of the scene for long."

"Alex is asking around the BDSM community." Luca slipped his phone into his inside suit pocket.

"We should go." Giada freshened her lipstick.

"Are we doing the delivery tonight?"

"Luca? No, tonight is with Edmond Story. He has a network of smurfs. Once you close the deal with Ferraro, we're going to need a larger network."

Money laundering. Smurfs were fodder, low level players to layer and integrate the mobs money back into the system.

They rode in silence to the restaurant. Carlo drove.

"Are you sure you're up to this?" Giada asked.

"Careful, you'll sound like you care."

"I care about the family—I protect my own interests," she said. "Lately, you've been in my way."

Luca chuckled. "Do you expect me to be sorry I'm an inconvenience to you?"

"No, because once this deal is done, and I return to Italy, you won't be my problem anymore."

"Good. Talk to Marco. Suck his dick until he gives you what you want."

She licked her lips. "It's worked in the past."

They pulled up to the restaurant downtown. Tuscany carried their label. Not only would they enjoy authentic Italian, but they'd be able to impress Edmond Story with their finest selection.

Luca rested his hand on Giada's lower back. Touching her made his flesh crawl. Carlo followed, staying diligent to avert any potential situations.

Edmond Story waited in the bar of the restaurant. Luca shook his hand. Giada pressed against Story, allowing him to rest his hand on her hip as he kissed both her cheeks.

"You are lovely this evening." He held his hand out to the table, indicating they should sit. "Join me for drinks?"

"My associate, Carlo."

"And my partner, Banks." A man nodded from the corner bistro table.

Carlo moved to the corner, spoke with Banks, and sat with him.

Luca took a seat. Beyond the bar, windows lined the wall. Traffic moved along the street.

Edmond held the chair for Giada. Tonight, Luca represented the chess piece in the game to show the intention of the Bruno family. Giada was the bait and the reward if Edmond wished to get his hands dirty in mob money.

The server approached. "A bottle of Bruno Twenty-Sixteen."

"Right away." The server scrambled off to find the eight-hundred-dollar bottle of wine.

Giada leaned in and flirted with Edmond. Her fingers tickled her earlobe, making the two carat studs in her ears catch the light. She was a cunt, but as brilliant as the diamond draped around her neck.

Wine was poured, Luca nodded and agreed where needed, but his thoughts were wandering the city, wondering where—who Mia really was.

A blonde woman in the corner laughed. Luca heard Mia's voice in his head. Saw her in women on the street. He narrowed his gaze at the black SUV across the street. He sat straighter, staring hard.

"Luca?"

"Excuse me." He rose from the table and approached the window.

Carlo came up beside him. "Is it Mia?"

A petite woman stood on the sidewalk with two men. Tension rolled over him, tightening his gut, stiffening his spine, and making the hairs on the back of his neck prickle. His gaze traveled the slim line of the woman's back. She had obvious wealth.

Designer clothes fit her form to perfection. Blonde hair tumbled around her neck and down her back. A gust of wind blew her hair over her shoulder. She quickly pulled it back around her neck, as if she had something to hide. If it was Mia, she did.

He froze. She moved like Mia, concealing her flesh. Flesh that, if she were Mia, bore the evidence of his hands and mouth. The tall, thin man with glasses shook her hand. A large man with arms as big as pythons stood protectively next to her.

Finally, the big man wrapped his arm around her. He opened the rear door for her. She turned, smiling up at the man, and then climbed into the car.

"Fuck. Stay with Giada."

Luca sprinted from the restaurant.

"Mia," he shouted.

Traffic kept him from being able to dart across the street. His gaze connected with the driver. Luca put his hand out to try and stop traffic. Taking a chance, he rushed into the street, but the SUV pulled away from the curb before Luca could reach him.

"Stop," he hollered as the SUV sped away.

A car blared its horn. Luca jogged across the street, bent at the waist, and gulped a breath.

Rage brewed in his gut, a fiery inferno of fucking pissed. He entered the building to find the man with the glasses.

There was a building directory inside the foyer. As he glanced down the list of names, his phone vibrated.

"Luca!" Giada spat. "Are you crazy?"

"Make my apologies. I'll be back as soon as I can. Be the boss bitch you are. Seal the deal without me. Just stay in the fucking restaurant with Carlo." He disconnected as his gaze narrowed on the name Grant Sutton and Associates. *Grant.*

Taking a chance that it was the Grant from her phone call, Luca strode down the hall to the glass door. He pushed it open. The man in the glasses glanced over to him.

"I apologize. We only take appointments."

"I have an appointment."

He straightened. "Excuse me?"

"You were just speaking to a blonde woman on the street."

The man swallowed but didn't speak.

Luca's chest tightened and burned. Unleashed fury curled his hands into fists. "Iris White?" No recognition of the name seemed to affect the man. The man's eyes didn't blink. "Mia Toliver?" His eyes widened. "So, it is Mia."

The man attempted to appear calm, but veins pulsed at his temples and sweat trickled along his hairline.

"Who is she? And where can I find her?" Luca spoke low and controlled, but inside he wanted to tear the man apart, ripping the truth from his mouth.

"I don't know who you're talking about."

Luca pulled his gun and pointed it at the man's head.

"Oh shit." Grant lifted his hands.

Luca closed the space between them. "I want her name and address. Be smart, Grant Sutton. Don't lie to me."

"What do you want with her?"

Now, they were getting somewhere. "Who is she and where can I find her?"

"Mia Hudson. I don't know who you are, and I don't want to. But you can't get to her."

"And the man she was with?"

"Her husband."

A smile curved his lips. "Husband?"

"That's all I know."

No, the man wasn't her husband. But that didn't mean this man was lying. "If you are lying to me, I will come back for you."

The man scratched a number on a piece of paper. "Here. It's her phone number. You want to talk to her, call her. I don't want any part of this."

Luca slipped the paper into his pocket and dropped the gun to his side.

"I assume you're going to call her. Tell her Luca is looking for her, and I will find her."

***

Mia's hand trembled as she lowered the phone to her lap. She looked at Hudson in the rearview mirror. "Take me to Protocol."

"No."

"You can come in with me. Please, I thought I could walk away but Luca isn't going to understand. I have to figure out another way. Hudson, I love him. I can't hurt him like this. No one at Protocol is going to give him answers, and Grant lied to him. He's going to tear apart anyone I know."

Hudson grunted. "Let's go."

Twenty minutes later, Mia slid her card through the door at High Protocol.

A fixture of the club, Joel sat at his station near the door. "Tinker? You look beautiful." He kissed her cheek.

"Is the Boss here?"

"Yeah." Joel's gaze collided with Hudson's. "What's up with all the bodyguards? Luca was in here yesterday with an armed escort."

"It's complicated." She nodded toward the door. "I'm going to go find Alex."

"You can. He can't. Not with the gun."

"Joel, it's me. It's important. Hudson won't leave my side." She sighed. "And he won't give up the gun." She fought the rising panic. She needed in the club. "Trust me. You want him to be the one with the gun if trouble follows me in here."

Joel nodded.

"Thank you. Listen," she said to Hudson. "Don't stare, don't judge, and please don't say anything. And don't shove people off me. These are my friends, my club. I know you don't understand, but I belong here."

He grumbled but nodded.

Inside the club, music set the tone. She tried to imagine the club from Hudson's perspective. Whips, latex, the scent of leather and sex. Her nipples hardened, and her body responded. She weaved her way to the observation platform, assuming Hudson would stay close behind.

She smiled at Chris behind the bar. She pointed to the platform, and he nodded. Opening the red rope barrier, she climbed the steps.

Ronan crossed the platform and pulled her into his arms. "Tinker. We've been waiting for you."

Alex slowly approached. His lips thinned, and his hooded gaze narrowed on her. Then he pulled her into his arms.

She sighed and settled into the comforting warmth of his arms.

"Let's go talk."

"Okay." She released a breath and gathered her strength.

Hudson blocked the exit with his arms folded.

Alex shifted her behind him, as if to protect her.

"He's with me," she said stepping around Alex.

"We can talk in the office," Alex said and walked ahead.

"You look beautiful, Tink." Ronan walked next to her, and Hudson followed.

Regrets welled within her, but also feelings of home. She'd lied for so long, her lies became her truth. Here she was Tinker.

Inside the office, the heavy weight of silence fell over the room.

Hudson blocked the door, Ronan leaned against the wall, and Alex sat behind the desk.

Alex lifted his hands and let them fall to the desk. "Tinker, who are you?"

She sighed and glanced over her shoulder to Hudson. He nodded.

"Mia Evangeline Thomas."

Alex leaned back, the leather of the chair creaking under his weight. "I guess I understand now why Iris White is a member of my club."

"Who?" Ronan asked.

The side door slammed open.

Hudson pulled his gun and aimed.

Tinker screamed at Hudson. "No!"

"What the fuck?" the Professor shouted.

"Are you fucking crazy?" Ronan put up his hands. "What the fuck is going on?"

"Stop." Panic laced her words. "Stop."

The Professor rounded the desk and pulled her into his arms. He lifted her off the ground, burying his face in her neck. He breathed deeply. "Where have you been?"

"I'm sorry. I know I made you worry."

"Fuck, Tink." He nuzzled her neck. "I thought that ass had hurt you."

"I'm fine."

He set her down.

"I promise, I'll come find you after I talk with Ronan and the Boss." She quickly pressed her lips to his. She'd once thought he didn't care, wasn't emotionally connected to anyone, but she could feel his love for her, her best friend. She hoped he understood why she wasn't sharing this with him when he believed she shared everything with him. "I need to talk to them privately."

The Professor's gaze shifted to Hudson. The gun lowered but remained in his hand, ready to defend her.

"Don't leave without finding me?" He kissed her forehead. "Don't fucking scare me like this again."

"I promise."

He left the room. Hudson re-holstered his gun.

Once they were alone, she told them all she could without breaking Luca's confidence. "Luca's looking for me. I'll find him and talk to him. I lied to him."

"You lied to us," Alex said.

"I know. Do you understand why?"

"No," Ronan said. "What am I missing?"

"Mia can't be in public without armed guards." Hudson crossed his arms over his chest. "The Thomas name has enemies, mostly in organized crime."

"Ronan, our Tinker is an heiress," Alex said. "A billionaire heiress."

Mia lowered her gaze.

"How does Luca fit into all of this?"

She swallowed. How did she explain without betraying the man she'd fallen in love with? She couldn't find the words.

"Tinker?" Alex asked.

"Yes." The one whispered word said everything. She'd given everything to him.

"I'll fucking kill him." Ronan paced across the room.

"Tinker? Was it your choice?" Alex asked.

Tears filled her eyes. "I've never felt this way about anyone. He's more than my Dom, Alex. He's killing me, who I was. My choice. What I wanted because I want to be what he needs." She launched from the chair. "He owns me. Owns my heart. I wanted to walk away from my life, become his slave, live as Tinker for the rest of my life. But I can't." She wiped tears from her cheek. "And I can't bring him into my world."

She snatched a tissue from the box on the side desk.

"What are they talking about?" Hudson asked her.

"I was a virgin. I slept with Luca."

"Christ, Mia," Hudson said. "The shit just keeps getting deeper. You're in bed with the fucking—"

"I know," she interrupted. "This is about me. Not Luca."

She turned back to Alex. "I need to stay away for a while. To be sure it's safe. If I come back, I'm just Tinker."

"If?" Ronan asked.

"When I come back." She smiled, but she didn't feel it. A weight settled in her chest. "I'm just Tinker."

Alex stood. "And if Luca shows up looking for you?"

"I'm going to talk to him. I'll go to his hotel tomorrow and explain." To tell him the truth and hope he understood. Otherwise, he was going to see her as his enemy.

"We should go," Hudson said, checking his watch. They weren't staying in one place too long.

Ronan hugged her again, pressing a kiss to her temple. "You know we don't care about your money. And we don't care if you're a virgin. We just want you to be safe."

"Safe, sane, and consensual." She smiled.

"You're special, Tink," Ronan said. "Gotta make sure the Dom who wins your heart deserves you."

"I need to talk to the Professor before I go."

Alex pointed to the door at the rear of his office. "Go through the back. And if you're worried about her safety," he said to Hudson, "you can take her out through my private entrance."

Hudson nodded.

Alex hugged her. "I'm here if you need me."

"I'll make sure you get my information. Just be sure to code it." Her gaze softened. "For your protection, too."

She weaved her way through the club. The Professor sat with Trinity.

"Oh my God, Tinker. Way too covered up." Trinity kissed her cheek.

"I'm not here to play tonight." Her gaze settled on the Professor. "Can we talk?"

He nodded and opened his arms. But she couldn't bring herself to sit on his lap. She wasn't his Tinker anymore.

"I'm going to take a walk," Trinity said. "Come on big guy. You're with me." She curled her fingers around Hudson's bicep.

Hudson didn't budge.

"Or not. See you later, Tinker." Trinity shuffled off.

"Is he going to pull a gun on me if I touch you?" the Professor asked.

Tinker leaned her head on his shoulder. "Thank you, Dario." She never called him by his name. "For being my friend. For never judging me. Not everyone understands me, but you do. That's why I love you."

He wrapped his arm around her shoulder. "Why does this sound like goodbye?"

"Maybe it is. I don't know. I just know I've been lying for so long I've forgotten the truth."

"And Luca?"

"Yeah, he was the one." She sighed. "He is the one. But I've lied to him, too."

"Are you going to tell me what's going on with you?"

"No, I can't. Just know I'm good."

"How good?" He arched one brow.

"I don't have anything to measure it against. That didn't come out right. He doesn't need measured."

The Professor laughed. "Are you going to tell me about it? You tell me everything else."

"God, but he's good with a belt."

"Ah, fuck. No," Hudson said. "No discussing this." He waved his finger around the room. "I don't want to hear about the kinky shit."

"I'm guessing he's not in the scene." The Professor wiped his hands on his thighs. "We could do a scene and show him what he's missing."

"He has a gun. He'll shoot you."

"Then don't tell him the shit I've done to you in the past."

"Never." She kissed his cheek. "I need to go."

"Be careful."

"Always. You've trained me well."

Chapter Eight

Luca nursed another tumbler of cognac. Grant had lied. He could go back and put a bullet in his head, but he'd only intended to square the truth out of him. He'd failed. The ballsy nerd lied right to his face with a gun at his head.

Giada slammed the door.

Carlo woke from his slumber, lifting his gun.

"Go back to sleep," she said. "You're useless." She stalked to Luca. "I found your girlfriend."

Carlo sat and spun his legs around.

"Where?" Luca set his drink to the side.

"I had an associate positioned at the sex club."

"She went to Protocol?"

"Ah yes, seems she still needed more than you could give her." She cocked one brow. "I know how she feels. She was there with her boyfriend or husband. Big guy, and he's packing."

"Fuck. Carlo, let's go."

"Calm down. She's not there. She slipped out undetected. I have my sources working on it." She picked up his tumbler and finished it. "Get some rest. We meet the buyer tomorrow. Early morning in the industrial district."

Giada sashayed into the adjoining suite.

Luca picked up his phone to call Alex.

"Maybe you should wait," Carlo said. "If she knows you've found her, she may run again. Never enter a situation without a plan. We still don't know where, or who, she is."

Luca was left to imagine Mia in the club, her body anchored to a cross, the blush of crimson to her flesh, and a wail of pleasure from her lips. Now, when she came, would she open her legs. Another fucking Giada. Only instead of money and power, she wanted pain and pleasure.

"Get some sleep," Luca said to Carlo. "I want to get this shit show over and send Giada home."

***

Luca woke early, showered, and dressed in dark gray suit. Giada stood at the windows of his suite.

"Why are you here?" Luca rolled his shoulders and poured a cup of coffee from the decanter.

"I like watching you sleep."

"Imagining I'm dead?"

She smiled and pulled a cigarette from the silver case in her hand. "Sometimes."

"When did you start smoking again?"

Her gaze shifted to his as she lit the cigarette. "Occasionally. When I feel powerful. You know, after good sex or when everything we want is right at our fingertips."

"We've moved diamonds before."

Her lips pursed. "I know. And it feels fucking incredible."

"Why the early drop?" From the rush to deliver to the timing of the exchange, everything about this deal felt off.

"Ask Marco."

He wasn't asking Marco. He wasn't going to speak to him at all.

She blew a stream of smoke into the air. "I found out the name of your girlfriend."

"Stay out of it, Giada."

"I'm afraid I can't. I've already called Marco and given him the name. You've been perfectly played."

Luca stood. "Who is she?"

"Mia Evangeline Thomas."

He crossed to the window. "Impossible." Nausea rolled through his gut. "Thomas? No."

"Yes. She played you."

No. She couldn't have known of his connection to her family. And what would she have gained from it? But then why had she lied about her name? His gut roiled. She had to have known.

"You're lying."

"You wish, but no, she's the endgame."

Was he a piece in whatever game she played?

He picked up the vase on the table and sent it flying into the wall. "That bitch!"

"You're a fool, Luca." Giada goaded him. "But it's over now. Marco will take care of it."

"Marco can stay the fuck out of my business. I'll handle Mia Thomas." He hadn't let an innocent into the lion's lair. He'd brought the enemy. Roberto had disposed of his competition. But when one head of the snake was cut, another was always there to take its place.

Once Giada left the room, Carlo pulled Luca aside. "Something isn't right, Luca. The woman you met in the club isn't a Mafia princess looking to even the score. No fucking way."

Luca scrubbed a hand over his face then stared hard at Carlo. "I don't know what to believe."

"Giada and Marco or Mia? You really don't know who to trust?"

No, because he couldn't trust himself.

"We make the exchange, then we find Mia."

"And if she's Mia Thomas?"

"I don't know. Nothing makes sense. She's with Ferraro."

Carlo checked his clip and holstered his weapon. "Stay alert. I don't feel good about this."

Giada strode back into the room. She checked the rounds in her revolver and slipped it into her purse. "Ready?"

"Give Carlo the diamonds."

"Why?" She tucked her purse close to her side.

"Because I said to. Don't fucking question my orders." Luca prowled closer. "Who the fuck do you think you are? Don't answer. You're Marco's and Roberto's whore. Maybe also Orlando's and Stefano's?"

She dug in her purse and tossed the bag to Carlo.

Luca nodded to Carlo. He opened the string and pulled a few stones from the pouch. "We're good."

"What? Do you doubt my loyalty?"

"Absolutely."

"Then watch your back."

Carlo grabbed her hair and yanked her back a few steps. When she stumbled, he closed his fingers around her throat. "Do you need me to remind you about loyalty?" He shoved the bag back in her purse.

"No, get your hands off me." She adjusted her clothes when he released her. "We need to go."

The first fingers of dawn touched the horizon as the vehicle pulled into the industrial park. Carlo parked near the two other cars in the parking lot of the two-story steel and cinderblock building.

"This is wrong," Luca said. "Too isolated. This isn't how we do business." Drops were made in hotel lobbies, bars—any public venue. Hell, he'd met cartel members in restaurants.

Giada's heels clicked on the sidewalk as they approached the building.

Inside the reception area, a woman sat behind a desk. She pressed a button, and the double doors to the left opened. "You're expected."

Two armed men waited with weapons in their hands.

Giada stepped forward.

Carlo rested a hand on Luca's forearm. "I can't let you go in." He pulled his gun from his holster. "You'll be too exposed."

If Carlo sensed a problem, sounding the alarm for vigilance, Luca took precautions. He always heeded Carlo's instincts. He gripped his gun.

"That would be a mistake," the voice came from the shadow of the room.

"Then tell your men to put their guns away," Luca said. "You're doing business with the Bruno family."

"The diamonds, please."

Luca lifted his gun. "Giada, step back."

"I'm afraid I can't. I have a delivery to make." She pulled the diamonds from her purse.

Bang! Shots rang out. Carlo cursed. Blood misted in the air. Luca squeezed off rounds as they lunged from the open doorway. Another shot came from the guard on the left. The woman at the desk pulled a weapon. Carlo spun, firing a shot, hitting her in the head.

Giada screamed, the woman's blood and brains splattering Giada's face.

Luca grabbed Carlo and surged out the door. Another round of shots followed. Bullets ricocheted off the ground. Cinderblock exploded as they ran around the corner of the building.

"Fuck!" Fire surged through Luca's leg. He braced against the building and scanned left and then right. "Where?"

Carlo held his palm over his bloodied arm. "We need cover."

They were too far from the vehicles. Fifteen seconds and they'd be out of options. Moving along the limited protection of the building, they checked the handles of parked vehicles.

Luca limped along. Blood gushed down his leg, flooded his shoe, and left an easy trail for them to be followed. The area was too open, and at this time of morning, too deserted.

They circled the building, taking cover behind the dumpster. Blood dripped onto the blacktop. Men searched the area.

"I think we're fucked," Carlo said.

Luca gritted his teeth against the pain tearing through his leg.

The door of the building swung open. Giada cursed at a large man gripping her arm. The man drew his hand back and struck her hard across the face. She stumbled, grabbing the car with one hand to keep from falling and cupping her jaw.

"Fuck you," she spat and flailed her arms.

The man pinned her against the car, his body crushed against hers, and he wrapped his fingers around her neck.

"Maybe he'll kill her." Carlo leaned against the dumpster.

Luca grunted. "If he doesn't, I will."

The man opened the car door and forced her into a vehicle with one of the other men.

A second man slashed the tires of Luca's car.

"Well, there goes our ride," Carlo muttered.

"Yeah, but it might still be our best shot at getting out of this shit." Bulletproof, dark tinted glass, and in plain sight.

"What about Giada? Is she involved?"

Luca glared at the car they'd pushed Giada into. "Possibly." With the way she'd sashayed into the room, she seemed ready for the fallout. Ignoring his orders to step back contributed to his doubts. "If the bitch is involved, she's dead."

"We don't know how many are inside?" Carlo said.

"We don't know how many she has on the outside either," Luca said. "If we were set up, she couldn't have planned it alone."

"Think she's working with someone in the family?"

Luca didn't know. But until he did, he couldn't trust any of his associates. He couldn't trust his family. "We're on our own."

The car drove away. Luca checked his clip. He was down to two shots plus the rounds in the weapon at his ankle. "How many rounds do you have?"

Carlo checked his gun. "I'm empty, but I have clips in the vehicle."

Their SUV might be their only chance. As soon as the area was clear, they made their move. Supporting Luca with his good arm, Carlo led the way to the vehicle

With quiet slowness, Carlo opened the back door. He protected Luca with his body, blocking the door, until Luca was inside. Carlo slid in beside him, locked the doors, and hunkered down.

For now, they were safe. "We sit tight," Luca said.

***

"How long are we going to wait?" Hudson paced in the hotel suite a few doors down from Luca's.

"I need to talk to him." Mia folded her hands in her lap.

"This is dangerous."

"I know. Trust me. I don't want to be anywhere near Giada. But I'm not afraid of Luca. He's going to be angry, but he won't hurt me."

Rustling sounded outside the door. Hudson held up a finger, telling her to be quiet. He listened. Outside the door, someone spoke Italian.

Hudson cocked his gun, kept it next to his thigh, and opened the door. "Excuse me," he said and closed the door.

"What?" Mia asked.

"Trouble. We need to get out of here."

Mia grabbed her purse and crossed to Hudson. "Who was out there?"

"A woman. Petite. Attractive. Dark hair."

"Giada."

"Yeah, she's wearing someone's blood."

"Oh my god, Luca."

"Mia, right now, you are my only worry." He stilled with his fingers on the door handle. "Shortest distance out is down the hallway and past their rooms. Stay on my right. Hopefully, if anyone is watching, my body will block most of you. The minute we turn the corner, we hit the stairwell."

She nodded.

"As we pass their door, in case they have someone watching, I want you to laugh and tuck your face into my shirt." The hard clench of his jaw softened. "Act like you're into me."

Hudson casually draped his arm around Mia as they exited the room.

But when it came time to laugh, she could barely manage a smile. Tears filled her eyes. Hudson laughed and pulled her tighter, giving her comfort, and letting her know it was okay. Once they rounded the corner, Hudson pulled his gun, popped open the stairwell door, and listened.

"Let's go."

Mia's scrambled to keep up as they rushed down the five flights of stairs. Rather than leaving through the lobby, Hudson led her down the hallway to one of the side, keycard entries.

"We have to find Luca."

"No." He grabbed her hand and pulled her along with him. "I'm getting you back to the estate where I know you're safe."

Mia ripped her hand from his. "Hudson, no. I need you." She was tired of being on the verge of crying. Why couldn't Hudson just listen to her and do what she asked? She felt as if she had to beg. He worked for her, and damnit, she was done cowering. "I need you to find Luca. Everything is so fucked up and I can't help feeling this is my fault."

"And I need to keep you safe. Our two needs aren't compatible. You are my priority."

"Yes, and he's mine. I'm not asking. I'm telling you. I have to know he's okay."

Hudson grunted and scanned the parking lot. "Can we fight about this once I have you safely in the vehicle?"

"We can fight. We can argue. I'll do whatever you say to keep me safe at the same time, but I need to see him with my own eyes to know he's not hurt. Maybe we should have stayed in the hotel room. He could be on his way here."

"The chick with the dark hair is wearing someone's blood. They're Mafia. I can tell you.

They don't like witnesses to their business dealings." He held the rear car door open for her. Then he went around the front of the vehicle and climbed behind the wheel.

Mia leaned into the front of the car. "Hudson. He's important."

"Fuck." He slammed his fist against the steering wheel. "You have no idea what you're getting into."

"Really? I was already in it! I know my parents are dead, probably at the hands of organized crime. I know my brother is gone because he couldn't deal with it. Do you think I haven't self-diagnosed my issues? Why I spend every night in a BDSM club? Why I sleep on the floor in a dungeon and wish for someone to save me from myself?"

He sighed. "I know, sweetheart." He combed his fingers through his beard. "Where do you think he could be?"

She shrugged. "He's here to deliver diamonds."

Hudson grunted again. "What's his cell number? Let's try calling him."

She didn't speak.

Hudson shifted on the seat.

"I don't know his number. Alex would, but I don't think we should involve anyone else. Obviously, someone has already been hurt. I used his phone to call Poppy last week. I told her to keep a record of the number."

Hudson started the car.

"Where are we going?" She glanced out the window.

"To find your boyfriend."

Twenty minutes later, they were with Poppy in the kitchen.

Mia's heart raced when Hudson handed her his phone. "Use my phone to call. I'm not letting him drag you any deeper into his shit."

She swallowed the extra saliva in her mouth. "I don't know what to say to him."

Sweat dampened her neck and trickled along her spine.

Hudson took the phone and started to enter the numbers.

"I'll call him." She snatched the phone from him. A cyclone of butterflies swirled in her belly. "Don't look at me."

Poppy hurried to the cupboard and pulled out a bottle of whiskey. She poured some in a tumbler, made the sign of the cross again, and drank.

Hudson took the seat next to her and stared into her eyes. "I'm staying right here."

She dialed the number and waited. One beat of her heart. Two. Three. Her heart thudded in her ears. The call connected. A ring and then another.

"*Pronto. Chi è,*" he answered in Italian.

Mia froze because his voice was hard and clipped. Her heart raced.

"Who is this?" he asked again.

She fought for a breath, then whispered. "It's Mia."

"*Bella*, where are you?" He groaned. "Listen, you shouldn't have called this number." Every word seemed labored to speak.

Fear clawed at her. He sounded as if he were in pain. "Where are you? Are you hurt?"

He groaned again and spoke in Italian to someone.

"Luca?"

"Give me the fucking phone." Hudson grabbed the phone from her hand and put it on speaker. "Listen up."

"Who is this? Leave her alone. If you hurt her, I'll kill you."

"Shut the fuck up and listen. Are you hurt?"

"Fuck you."

"Luca! Listen to him. He can help."

"I saw your partner covered in blood," Hudson said. "Is it yours?"

Luca gasped into the phone. "No, but I have a bullet in the leg. My consigliere took a hit to the arm."

Mia gulped and tears sprang to her eyes.

"How long ago?" Hudson asked.

"Thirty minutes maybe longer."

"Location."

"Unknown. We were in the industrial park, East side. We're in the back seat of our vehicle."

"Friendly?"

"No, definitely not friendly. And our vehicle has been disabled. It's being towed."

"Leave your phone on and keep it with you. I'll track you to your location."

"Who are you?"

"I'm the one coming to get you. We'll discuss more face to face."

Hudson disconnected before Mia could say more.

"What now? How will you find him?"

"I'll track his phone. Don't ask me how. You're in enough shit, and you don't need to get buried under mine, too."

"Am I the only one who obeys speed limits and doesn't break the law?" Poppy mopped her brow with her arm. "Oh, fine. I go to illegal bingo on Sunday nights. I won two hundred dollars last week." She went for another drink. "Now, we all go to hell together."

Mia followed Hudson out to the garage to the vehicles. He opened the rear of the black SUV, opened the floor compartment, and retrieved a duffel bag. He opened the zipper and dug through the supplies. Not only did he carry guns with silencers, long range sniper scopes, ammunition, tactical clothing, binoculars, knives, and electronic equipment, but he also pulled out a Kevlar vest and shrugged it on.

"Send the staff home, Mia. Tell them you're going out of town and give them the week off. Just

Poppy. I don't want her here either, but she's not going to leave you. Guards are on alert."

"I want to come with you." She needed to have her hands on Luca, to have his hands on her, to feel his heart beat beneath her fingertips.

"I need you to stay here. Once I get to him, I can triage his injuries, but he's going to need medical."

"He won't go to the hospital. They'll ask questions."

He kissed her cheek. "I'll bring him home." He smiled. "Hopefully, I won't have to kill him once I get him here."

***

Luca tightened the tourniquet on Carlo's arm. Blood soaked his shirt, dripped from the wound, and pooled beneath him. He leaned against the door. Color had drained from his face. "What did she say?"

"Not much." Luca replayed the conversation in his mind. "I don't know what to think. But I know we aren't going to last in here."

"Where do you think they're taking us?" Carlo reloaded his guns.

"They don't know they have us. They're just getting the vehicle out of sight." They had bodies and bullet holes to contend with. Hopefully, tomorrow they wouldn't find two dead Italians in the backseat.

The car jerked to a stop. Break lights ahead lit the interior.

"Shh." Luca lifted just enough to peer out the side window. They stayed low enough in the back so as not to be seen if anyone looked through the front windshield. A man exited the tow truck.

"Contain this," another man said.

"We tagged them both. I've got associates watching the hospitals. When they show up, and they will, we'll take care of it."

"We were double crossed. How else would they know to have another car waiting?" The voices faded as they moved farther away.

Luca breathed a little easier. "They think we split."

"I need a doctor." Carlo's gaze took in the bloody pants clinging to Luca's thigh. "So do you."

"I know."

He checked his phone. Twenty minutes had passed since Mia called.

"Did she say why she ran?"

Luca shook his head. Was the man with Mia when she'd called the same man from the black SUV? Too many unanswered questions lingered in his mind. Mia would have the answers. He'd get them even if he had to punish her to get to the truth.

Carlo's eyes drifted closed.

"Stay with me." Luca felt his neck. His pulse was strong, and his flesh still warm.

"I'm not dead," he said with a laugh. "We should talk now while we still have privacy."

Carlo opened his eyes and stared hard at Luca. "Listen to her before you accuse her of anything."

"I will get to the truth, Carlo. If Giada and Marco set this up, there will be war within the Bruno family."

"And if you discover Mia is involved?"

"Then I guess the war never ended."

Luca's phone rang. "Mia?"

"No. Don't fucking shoot me. I'm two minutes out."

The call disconnected. Luca's pulse jumped. Adrenaline surged. He held his gun with his finger poised to slide to the trigger. He wouldn't shoot, but he was going to make sure Mia's associate was friend not foe before he lowered his weapon.

A rattle sounded outside the vehicle. Luca held his finger to his lips and aimed his gun. Both hunched lower in the seat.

"Unlock the door," the man outside the car whispered.

Carlo hit the unlock button, the door opened, and Luca pointed his weapon.

"What the fuck?" the huge man rasped. The same man that had driven Mia in the black SUV. "Put the gun away. I counted four. I figure we've got about thirty seconds to get out of here." He hauled Carlo out of the vehicle like a sack of potatoes and braced him against the side of the car.

Luca lowered his gun and slid across the seat, taking his chances with Mia's *husband*. If he did intend to kill Luca, it wouldn't matter. He was dead either way.

The man peered into the backseat of the vehicle. "Good."

"What?"

"Talk later. E and E."

Luca furrowed his brow. "Is that English?"

"Escape and Evade. Keep an eye on our six. Weapon ready. I've got you, so you're going to have to take out any adversaries. No one is friendly." The man banded one arm around Luca and the other around Carlo. They quietly made their way from the building.

Outside, the sun was high and hot. Luca squinted against the blinding rays. He kept his gaze locked to the right and behind. Carlo kept watch on the left. Another fifty yards and they'd be at the vehicle. Twenty-five.

Carlo moaned.

"Hang tight. Almost there."

Luca opened the back driver door.

"Help Carlo first," Luca said.

"Just get in the fucking car." The man thrust Luca into the vehicle, turning his back on their surroundings.

Shots fired from the left.

Carlo tensed, stepped in front of the man helping them, raised his weapon, and pulled the trigger. One man dropped.

"Fuck." The big man moved fast. He whipped around, gun in hand, firing a shot as he tossed Carlo into the car as if the two-hundred-pound Italian was a twelve-year-old boy. The second man crumbled to the ground, still aiming his gun and firing.

"Stay down," Mia's man yelled, throwing the car into drive. Tires squealed, the stench of burnt rubber filling the car. A hard right turn threw Luca into Carlo.

Carlo gasped with pain. "Fuck, he's strong." He laughed as he curled into a sitting position, holding his arm. The vehicle raced away from the scene.

Luca spoke to Carlo in Italian. "I wonder what she has told him about me. I don't know who to trust, Carlo. Can I trust Mia?"

"Do you have a choice?" Carlo twisted his wrist, aiming the gun at the driver. "Would you have left your enemy armed?"

Luca's chest tightened. "No, I would have left him dead."

"Hudson." The man spoke into an earpiece. "Twenty minutes. We're going to need medical." A pause. "Fuck, Mia, what do you mean you covered it?" He grunted. "You and I are going to have a little chat about following my orders."

Luca bristled. The only orders Mia would be following were his.

"You and I are going to have a chat," the man called Hudson said to Luca.

"Hudson?"

"Yep. First, you're going to stay the fuck away from Mia. I promised her I'd find you. And I did. But I didn't promise I wouldn't fucking take you back out. Your name doesn't mean shit to me." He took a deep breath. "But she means everything to me. I don't care where you go as long as it's fucking far from her."

Luca sat straight in the seat. No one threatened him. And no one took what was his. "Careful, friend."

"I don't need your warnings, and I'm not your friend."

Luca leaned his head back against the seat, closed his eyes, and silently cursed. American muscle, clearly ex-military, and protective of Mia. Protective he understood. Luca had been betrayed. All he had left to trust in was Carlo and his gut. And in his gut, he knew it wasn't Mia who betrayed him.

"On Mia, we are the same. I don't want her hurt." He swallowed, his mouth dry and gritty like sand.

They approached an electronic fence with armed guards. Luca's gut tightened. It was true. She was Mia Thomas. But did she know she was his enemy?

Or that he was hers?

***

Mia paced in the foyer with the front door open, waiting for the SUV to come charging up the drive. Footsteps sounded behind her. She turned and smiled. She wasn't alone in this. Poppy prayed and cooked. Hudson rushed off to the rescue, and she made a call to the person she knew could save Luca and Carlo and keep her secrets.

Dr. Brooks Leighton was a friend to High Protocol, a sadist Dom with experience treating patients in settings away from the scrutiny of hospitals. Law enforcement didn't always understand the BDSM community.

Brooks and Mia had history together. But as Tinker, Mia had experiences with most of the Doms at Protocol. That's what she did. Until Luca.

"When I got your call, this wasn't what I expected." Brooks waved his hand to the house and gardens.

She squinted into the distance. "I know. No one knows." She glanced to him. "Except Alex and Ronan. I mean, they know now. I told them." But they didn't know everything. "They don't know about Luca and his associates."

"What am I getting involved with, Tinker?" He leaned against the porch pillar. "Do I really want to know?"

"No one will ever know you were here." She'd protect him. But she needed him to save Luca. "Have you heard of the Bruno Family?" She took a breath. "I won't lie to you. They're Mafiosi."

"Tinker." He tilted his head and gave her a hard look. "I run a family practice."

"But you came from South Florida. I know you worked with unsavory associates."

"Not really and I left to get away from this shit."

"They're here." The black SUV came tearing up the drive and skidded to a halt in front of the house.

Brooks rushed ahead. Mia scrambled after him. He had the rear passenger door open. Hudson opened the rear driver's side door.

Mia stood a few feet back, her arms crossed over her chest, and stayed out of their way. Right now, Brooks and Hudson needed room to work. "Brooks, this is Hudson."

Brooks gave a cursory glance to Carlo's arm.

"That guy has a shot to the arm," Hudson said. "This one took a slug to the leg."

Brooks wrapped an arm around Carlo's waist and helped him from the car. "Let's get them inside."

Sticky blood covered Carlo's hand, plastered his clothes to his body, and smeared across his face. Spinning away from the car, his gaze found Mia. "Wait," he said as Brooks helped him hobble past. "Thank you," he whispered. He leaned forward and kissed her cheek.

"Put him in my bed," Mia said. She'd already shown Brooks where he could work on their injuries.

"This isn't simple stitches, Tinker. I'll see what I can do, but I'm not a surgeon."

Luca clung to Hudson, Italian spewing from his lips.

Carlo responded and chuckled. "He doesn't want me in your bed." He wiggled the fingers on the hand that still moved. "I told him I still have one good hand."

Mia was saved from responding as Brooks helped him into the house.

Luca winced, unable to put any weight on his leg. Mia's heart pounded. Fear and relief warred within her. How could he look so good when his pants, stiff and thick with blood, molded to his leg? He was covered in blood.

Hudson hauled him into the house. Mia followed.

Once he had Carlo in the bed, Brooks rushed down the stairs. Together, he and Hudson lifted Luca, protecting his injured leg and carried him upstairs. Inside her room, Brooks nodded toward the double doors. Hudson carried Luca into her dungeon and laid him out on the bed.

Mia waited just outside the dungeon. She couldn't go in.

Brooks gave Poppy instructions. She nodded and began removing Luca's shoes.

Hudson returned to Mia and rested his hands on her shoulders. "We need to talk."

She glanced to Brooks. He took a pair of scissors and began cutting the pant leg from Luca.

Hudson turned her and escorted her from the room, out into the hallway. "This is serious shit, Mia." He leaned against the wall and tipped his head back. "I haven't taken live fire since Afghanistan."

Mia sucked in a breath. "They were shooting at you? They knew you were coming to help. They must not have known it was you."

He laughed. "Not your boyfriend, but the people he pissed off." His gaze met hers. "You can't trust him."

Hudson was wrong. She couldn't do anything but trust him. "I made a mistake when I walked away from him. I can't do it again." She rested her hand on Hudson's arm. "I love him."

She didn't say more. Luca needed her as much as she needed him. After walking back into the bedroom, she sat on the edge of the bed next to Carlo. "Can I do anything to help?"

"I told your doctor to take care of Luca first. I'm good."

Mia stared at his arm. "You're hurt."

Carlo was quiet. "He's angry, Mia. He doesn't understand why you left…why you lied to him."

She nodded. "I know."

"Don't be afraid to tell him the truth."

Poppy carried a bowl of bloody water into the bathroom.

"Do you want a glass of water?" Mia asked Carlo.

"No, *bella*. I need whiskey and a cigarette."

She smiled. "I'll ask Brooks if that's allowed."

He groaned and cursed in Italian.

"Yeah, probably not going to happen. But once Brooks stitches you up, I'll sneak you out to the patio for a smoke." She was quiet. "I don't know what to say to him. Or if I should go to him."

"You're his submissive. That kinky motherfucker wants you to do what you're told."

"Think he'll punish me for lying to him?"

Carlo laughed, a rich, robust, explosion of sound. "Does he need a reason?"

Poppy shooed Mia away. "Brooks has orders. I need to start washing the blood off." Her gaze narrowed on Mia. "All the men in your life are too bossy."

Mia slid from the bed and crossed the room. She waited at the threshold to the dungeon but didn't enter. She couldn't go in, not with him lying there helpless.

Brooks sat on a chair next to the bed. He'd cut Luca's pants from his body, leaving him in his boxers. She wasn't sure if his shirt had been cut from him or if he'd just taken it off, but his bronzed chest rippled with excruciating breaths. His body trembled…and so did Mia.

Brooks had cleaned the wound, but the heavy stench of blood hung in the air. He'd dragged her spanking bench close to where he worked, his tools laid out on a sterile pad.

"You're lucky. Looks like a hole from a .22 caliber." He loaded a syringe and injected the tissue around the wound.

Nausea churned in her belly, and tears slid down her cheeks. She lowered her head, listening to Luca groan as Brooks leveraged higher, digging into the bullet hole to retrieve the slug. Blood oozed from the wound. Hudson took position across from him and used his military training to assist Brooks.

Brooks issued instructions to Hudson. "He should be in surgery," he said and dropped the slug to the sterile pad, "in a hospital."

He used a surgical cauterizer to stop bleeders. Blood puddled in the wound. Hudson soaked it up with more gauze.

"How are you doing?" Brooks asked Luca.

"I'll survive."

She prayed for his words to be true. So much blood. Nausea churned in her belly.

Mia lifted her gaze to find Luca staring at her from the bed.

"Do you want to come in," Hudson asked her.

Brooks laughed.

"Something funny, Doc?"

"I'm guessing you've never been in this room with her before," he said. "If you had, you wouldn't have asked. Tinker is told what to do."

Luca stiffened.

"Relax, Luca." Brooks wiped the wound with gauze. "Bleeding has stopped," he said to Hudson. "I just need to stitch him up."

Mia listened to them talk, but her gaze never wavered from Luca. His lips formed a hard line and his whiskey-colored eyes darkened. Pain etched into the face of the man she loved. A tear slipped onto her cheek.

She swallowed, needing to be next to him, to touch him. But he was in the dungeon, and she was his submissive.

Standing at the threshold, her arms hung at her side. And she waited for him to want her.

Luca spoke in Italian. She didn't know what he said, but the tone of his voice seeped into her. "Mia, *amore*."

Without hesitation, she stripped off her shirt, folded it, and set it on the floor. Next, she removed her loose pants.

"Mia, what the fuck are you doing?" Hudson lurched from the bed.

She was serving her Master.

"Leave her," Brooks said. "He might have been shot. He still won't let you touch his submissive."

"What the fuck? Mia?"

Brooks laughed as he set another stitch. "I'm guessing she's not allowed in a dungeon with clothes on." He tied off the stitch.

"He can't want us seeing her naked."

Brooks glanced up. "How well do you know Tinker?"

"You know a submissive named Tinker," Hudson said. "I know Mia."

"And he knows both." Brooks used a scalpel to clean the edges of the wound.

Mia walked across the room, naked, and stood next to the bed on the opposite side of where Brooks worked. Breath arrested in her chest. All that mattered was the man on the bed. This wasn't about who she'd been. But who she was with him.

Luca opened his arm, and she climbed onto the bed, curling into his side. Luca's blood-stained hand fisted in her hair. His grip tightened, pulling her closer. His eyes closed, and he buried his face in her hair, breathing in her scent.

"Fuck, Mia." Hudson grabbed the thin sheet folded on her slave mat on the floor at the end of the bed. He covered her nudity.

Mia rested her head on Luca's chest. "I'm sorry," she whispered.

Luca lifted her chin and slid his lips against hers. He groaned, pushing the sheet from her body. His hold on her intensified as he braced a hand on her back and pressed her intimately closer.

Hudson grumbled. "Are we about done here, Doc?"

"Yes." He covered the stitches with salve and a sterile bandage. Then he wiped his hands on a towel and stood. "Tinker, be gentle."

"Need help with Carlo?" Hudson asked.

Brooks nodded. "They're both going to be laid up for a few days. Are you sticking around?"

"I'm not going anywhere."

Their voices faded as they went to the other room.

Mia pressed a kiss to his sternum.

"Why?" he asked.

Her heart rattled in her chest. She thought of Carlo's words. "Because I was scared."

He grunted as he repositioned, sitting against the steel headboard.

"Of Hudson?"

Her brow pinched. "No." She leaned against him. "No," she softly said. "Of you."

"I would never hurt you, Mia."

"You were never supposed to know Mia."

Chapter Nine

Luca closed his eyes. Pain throbbed through his leg. Mia's hand rested on his stomach as she leaned against him. Once she started speaking, the words continued to tumble from her lips.

Her childhood, her brother, parents and living in fear. Nowhere in her story was his family mentioned.

"What happened to your parents?"

"No one is sure. They were in western Africa on business when they were taken hostage. The company paid the ransom, but they still didn't come home." She sighed. "Hudson tried to find out more, but he said we'd need an army of black op mercenaries to get the men who killed them. They'd still be gone." She sat and stared into his eyes. "Luca, I'm scared to be involved in another crime family. Mine are all dead."

"I'm selfish, Mia. I'll keep you in a tower to have you."

But he had hidden enemies, and he wasn't sure if they were within his own family. Even in a tower, could he keep her safe? He'd been unprepared for today. His defenses had been down, distracted by his obsession for her. She wanted owned. Good. He couldn't let anyone else have her.

"No one takes what belongs to me." He kissed her, sliding his tongue into her mouth. Fire slipped through his veins. He'd lost her once. Never again. "You won't run from me, Mia."

He palmed her breast, teasing her nipple into a hard point.

She moaned and shivered as he cupped her cunt, the cream of her arousal wetting his palm.

"A submissive with her own dungeon. Who do you bring here? The doctor?" He slid his fingers along the seam of her pussy. "Hudson?"

"No one. I've been waiting for you."

Luca stilled. Her words echoed his thoughts. "Are you mine?" He wouldn't just own her submission. He'd demand her obedience, her trust, and her fidelity. "Only mine?"

"Yes." She gasped a breath as she gripped his wrist. His finger slipped inside of her. Then two. Sliding into her wet sheath, he curved his fingers into her G-spot, drawing pleasure she was only just discovering.

"I won't share you." He stared hard into her eyes. "No one will touch you. I will kill anyone who attempts to take you from me."

"I'm yours, Luca."

He winced as he lifted his hips and pushed his boxers down. "I need inside you."

"You can't. You're hurt."

Luca fisted his hard cock. Pre-cum slicked the head. He gave it a slow stroke. "You should know, *bella*. A little pain is always better with the pleasure." Grabbing her thigh, he urged her over his lap.

Mia whimpered as her inner tissues stretched, welcoming him into her hot, tight core. Velvet heat surrounded him, her wet walls gloving to his shaft until the head bumped her cervix. Then he clenched his buttocks and pressed a fraction deeper. Her smooth flesh pliant against his sucked him in, an erotic friction sending shards of pleasure through him.

Luca gripped her hips hard, fingers digging into her, rocking her on his lap. Pain flared through his leg. He fought a wave of blackness, needing her more than he needed to rest.

"Luca, can I come?"

Desperation settled in his chest, an ache to feel her body convulse around his, to see his cock wet with her cream, to confirm she was safe in his arms. "Come, Mia."

She cried out, her body shuddering with a riot of quivering pulses. Her nails clawed his chest as she braced against him, lifting, lowering, and grinding against her release.

"Mia!" Poppy tsked as she pulled the door closed.

"Fuck!" Luca erupted, claiming her body with his, marking her with his mouth and his scent. Hot jets of cum pumped through his shaft, slicking her tight, fluttering channel. He thrust, wanting into the deepest part of her.

"I love you," she said, her voice trembling and soft. She gently collapsed onto his chest.

Luca banded his arms around her. He growled as he slathered kisses along her jaw. He sucked her neck, assuring he left her marked. "I love you, too, *amore mio*."

With enemies at his back, his love would put her in danger.

***

A couple hours later, Luca sat at the patio table overlooking Mia's estate. He'd believed he could impress her with gifts of clothing, private jets, and arrogance.

Mia could bury his family with her wealth, but she would be nothing against their power...their vengeance. The Bruno family carnage had already butchered her parents, destroyed her brother, but he vowed they would take nothing else from her.

Brooks sipped a cup of coffee. His eyes drooped. Blood stained his clothing. Luca didn't know him, didn't trust him. Mia did. The doctor hadn't asked questions. Carlo needed rest. He was sedated—in Mia's bed.

"Who put the hit on you?" Hudson's voice broke the silence.

Luca had his leg propped on a chair. His gaze shifted from Mia to Hudson. "I don't know yet. But I will find out."

"I took .22 slugs out of both of you." Brooks opened his tired eyes. "Hudson has them. I don't know what shit you're into, but my part is done. I'm here for Tinker." He smiled across the table at her. "She knows one call will have an army of protection around her."

"She doesn't need an army," Hudson said. "She has me."

Luca shook his head. And he thought he'd only have the bald Dom in the dungeon to worry about. Maybe Alex and Ronan. He wasn't surprised at the loyalty of those around her. Even Carlo had been ensnared by her charm.

"A real threat wouldn't have used a .22," Hudson said.

Luca's jaw clenched. A dark-haired Italian cunt, with a terrible shot, carried a pocket-sized semi loaded with twenty-twos. He'd assumed she'd pulled the diamonds from her purse, but he couldn't be sure it wasn't her gun. Was Marco involved? Giada didn't make a move without him.

"I'm giving you two choices," Hudson said. "I've already spoken to Mia."

Luca draped a hand across her thighs. "I'm listening."

"Mia's jet is ready. Get on it, get the fuck away from her, and stay gone. You and your Mafia family aren't getting near her."

Mia's gentle fingers closed over his.

"And my second choice?"

"I kill you."

The table grew quiet.

"Listen," the big guy continued, "there is enough blood in your vehicle to warrant a homicide investigation. But twenty-four hours from now, that SUV will disappear and any evidence in that building is going to vanish like smoke in the wind. I make one call, and this situation blows up. You'll be prime time news. Presumed dead. Italian Mafia hits close to home."

Luca raked his fingers through his hair. Fuck. Fuck!

"Luca, whoever wants you dead won't stop." Mia's eyes reflected the concern making her voice quaver. "You can stay here. You'll be safe, and it will give you and Carlo time to plan your next move."

"I lose everything. My family, my home, my country." His gaze hardened. "What of Savio?"

Hudson leaned back in his chair. "No choice comes without sacrifice."

Mia laced her fingers with his. "You will have me. And Hudson. We have resources."

Hudson grunted.

"Ignore him. That's his way of agreeing when he doesn't want to."

Luca glanced to Hudson, then to Mia.

"Say the words, Luca," Hudson said. "Once I make the call, Luca Bruno is dead."

Two choices? He had no choice.

Chapter Ten

Mia snuggled beneath the blanket. Luca's scent surrounded her, saturated the air between them. His soft measured breaths used to lull her to sleep. Tonight, like last night and the night before, the even tempo widened the chasm.

Her heart hurt. She hurt for the man who swore fealty to his family.

Last week, Hudson had made the call, police had descended on the industrial park, and Luca Bruno was presumed dead.

In her mind, the situation gave Luca the opportunity to investigate the treachery in his family from a distance. Protected. She had money and resources. He had a dark need for revenge. Her pulse jumped because someone had tried to kill Luca.

He'd died anyway. The man she'd fallen in love with was slipping further away.

There was distance between him and his family now. She hadn't been prepared for the distance growing between them. And she didn't know how to be strong for him. He didn't show weakness, especially when faced with betrayal.

Such was a man with honor, even if not everyone would understand the moral values of a Mafioso.

She closed her eyes as a tear slipped onto her cheek. He hadn't touched her, hadn't commanded her obedience. Each day he spoke to her less.

It was only here, at night, when he believed her asleep, did he speak to her. And then it was in Italian. She didn't need to understand the language to know she was losing him as he lost himself.

"Luca? Talk to me."

She rolled toward him. This wasn't the dungeon. She could touch him, but she wouldn't survive his rejection. In the darkness of her submission, she hadn't just given him her virginity, she'd given him her heart.

All she had now were the things she never wanted. Money, power, influence. All the things Luca had given up. What she desperately needed from him—his love, dominance, and control—had died with him.

"Go to sleep, Mia."

It was the closest thing to a command she was going to get. She closed her eyes and tried to sleep. In the twilight of consciousness, she felt his fingertips on her face.

"*Mi dispiace.*"

She'd heard those words before. She was sorry too. Sorry she didn't know what to say to him. Sorry she didn't know what he needed. And she was sorry she couldn't give him the one thing he seemed to want—the life he gave up. Was he sorry he had her and not his Mafia family?

***

In the morning, she sat with him next to the pool. Insecurity churned in her belly. Luca's leg was healing. Time was on his side now. He could begin unraveling the knots of deception and figure out a way to return to his life or decide to build a new one.

"Hudson has set up a secured network. He has a source that can access banking information and government agencies, even in Italy. He's working on getting a clone on Giada's and Marco's phones so you can get a log of their phone calls."

"He's taking care of everything." His gaze narrowed. "He's getting stronger."

"Carlo?"

"*Sì.*" Luca squinted into the distance. Carlo and Hudson moved in synchronized stretches, a form of martial arts, honing their bodies, and sharpening their combat skills.

Mia turned her gaze to his. "Are you?"

"Am I what?"

"Getting stronger."

"I don't know what I am anymore."

She remembered the feeling well. When everything familiar was suddenly stripped away. She'd found her escape in BDSM. High Protocol had become her sanctuary.

That was gone now, too.

Because Luca Bruno was assumed dead, his connection to Alex and the club died with him. And she belonged to Luca. His loss was hers. She swallowed the ache, burying it deep inside, where she kept her memories of Oliver and her parents. Another loss. Another heartbreak. Only this time she didn't suffer alone. They both drowned in their regrets. Both lost their purpose.

"What is happening to us?" Her throat tightened.

Gone was the arrogant Dom who'd once denied her pleasure, the man who seeped danger from his pours, and commanded her obedience.

"We've changed." He pushed off from the chair, and still with a slight limp, moved a few steps from her. "You are Mia Thomas, and I am without a name, without a family."

If he looked, he would see she desperately ached to be his family the way he'd become hers. She needed him.

Knots coiled in her belly. The man who could cut her to the core with a look simmered in his own dark thoughts.

"I feel useless here." He shoved his hands into his pockets.

His words broke her.

"You and Carlo will have new identities in a few weeks. You'll be able to leave the estate. I'll be sure you have the money you need." She fought the emotions boiling inside her, pressurizing, ready to erupt and destroy the little worth she had left.

She scooted her chair back and scampered toward the house.

"You want me to leave?"

She stumbled in her steps, desperately needing what he seemed incapable or unwilling to giving her. She shook her head. "It doesn't matter what I want, not anymore."

She continued into the house. Tears burned behind her eyes as she rushed up the stairs to her room. Carlo had been given a spare room farther down the hall.

She stared at her bed. She ached for what they had in Italy, for what they'd lost here in her house, a house that had stolen all of her dreams.

For the last week, he'd slept next to her, naked. Gentle caresses and whispered words in Italian. Nothing more. No intimacy. No sex. No discipline.

Tightness gripped her chest, her throat, and twisted within her as she turned to the closed dungeon doors, the last place he'd sought her submission. The day of the shooting. The last time she'd glimpsed the powerful Mafioso. The day Brooks removed the bullet, and Hudson demanded his death.

She could see now Luca should have gone back to his family in Italy. He chose death and now couldn't stand to be with her. An ache pierced her heart. She loved him enough to let him go.

"You didn't answer my question, Mia."

She spun at the sound of his voice.

He leaned against the doorjamb. His eyes darkened. "Are you having regrets?"

Tears filled her eyes. "Regrets? Yes. I have regrets." She crossed her arms over her chest like a shield, trying to protect her heart from the pain only he could inflict. "I'm so sorry, Luca. I know you do, too."

His gaze focused on her, rage swirling in his whiskey-colored irises. "I have only one."

His confession ripped the breath from her lungs. She was his regret, and for her, he was the one thing she could never regret. "I'm sorry I came into your life."

Luca roared and cleared her dresser with a sweep of his arms. "Is that what you believe? That my regret is you?"

She covered her face with her hands. Tears burst from her eyes. "I don't know what to do for you. I don't know how to fix this. I'm trying."

"I don't want you to fix this." His jaw clenched. He slammed his fist into the wall. Skin split on his knuckles. He drew in a heavy breath. "You can't."

"You only see Mia Thomas when you look at me."

"Because of who I am." He raked his fingers through his hair. "I am my Mafia family.

Their sins are mine. The Bruno family destroys their enemies. They'll destroy what's left of your family. I'll destroy you."

"I don't believe that. You own me," she cried.

An incredulous laugh bubbled from his lips. "And when you discover the truth, that my family takes and takes until you are left with nothing."

"I'm yours. What do *you* want?"

"You. Your love, your life, your future." His voice cut life a knife to her heart. "Even after you learn my every dark secret, I won't let you go."

She froze.

Tension rippled his muscles. The edge of his jaw hardened even more. "I want you, and I want your obedience."

Her chest rose and fell with sharp breaths. She licked her lips. "I gave you the only thing I cared about, the only thing I held sacred. You want anything else from me, it's yours."

His gaze narrowed. "Mia."

"Tinker." She didn't want to be Mia. Not here, not with him. His identity had been stripped from him, but not his power and control. "Sir, please."

He growled and stepped closer. For a moment, he stared at her, a predator hungry for his prey. He wrapped his fingers around her neck.

The feel of his fingertips sending shivers of delicious fear over her.

"I've already taken more than you'll ever know. Don't misconstrue my intentions. I'll take everything from you."

She remembered well. Ruthless and cruel. But he loved her, cherished her submission. He gave up his life to be with her.

Moisture slicked her folds. Her need for his dominance never sated.

"Please." She licked her lips.

"Crawl."

Mia dropped to her hands and knees and followed him to the dungeon. She stopped at the threshold, waiting for his permission to undress. Anticipation zinged along her spine. With all the insecurity surrounding them, this she understood.

Luca jerked off his shirt and tossed it to the bed. He stared at her.

"Strip."

Mia stood and quickly shed her clothing, neatly folding them, and leaving them by the door.

Luca approached her. He tunneled his fingers into her hair. "This is our dungeon now, but you will not enter without my permission." He cupped her pussy. "Mine. For my pleasure." He slammed his lips onto hers, demanding entrance, driving his tongue into her mouth.

She whimpered, pressing close to him, loving the feel of crisp hairs on his chest against her sensitive breasts.

He broke the kiss, resting his forehead against hers. "And this is yours." He held her hand against his flesh over his heart. He pressed his lips to hers, and this time, his kiss was a sweet possession of tongue and lips. Gentle nips followed delicious touches of his tongue to hers.

He spoke against her lips. "I want you over my lap, but for now, we'll settle for the bench. Braid your hair."

"Yes, Sir." After grabbing a tie from the dresser, she quickly fingered her hair into a braid.

Luca walked the perimeter of the room. He opened drawers and cabinets. Everything in the room was untouched until now. He stroked a thick rattan cane.

Her heart thudded. And then, when he set the cane aside, her heart hiccupped. She needed for the sting of the cane followed by the deep ache in her muscles.

Desire, hot and fierce, blazed through her. Luca selected an eighteen-inch leather flogger. His fingers sifted through the fall. Diamonds in the lion head ring on his hand glinted in the soft light as he gripped the handle.

He set the flogger to the side. When he turned, he held a lace-up, single sheath, forearm binder. He caressed the butter-soft leather as he approached her. Steely determination darkened his eyes and cut the hard line of his jaw.

"Your safeword?"

"*Rossa.*"

"Arms behind your back."

Her shoulder blades pinched together. Luca slid the binder up her arms, the leather encasing her from wrist to elbow. He tightened the laces. Her pulse fluttered. To keep the harness anchored, two leather straps wrapped over her shoulders, crossed her chest, tucked under her armpits, and joined again, attaching at the binder.

Luca held her shoulders as she knelt on the pads and flattened her chest along the table section of the bench. Adrenaline surged through her. Neoprene straps banded her legs, and another crossed over her hips.

His dungeon. His submissive. Restrained and under his command. Shivers chased over her flesh. This would be her sanctuary now, with the man who owned her.

Standing at the foot of the bench, he palmed her ass, running his hands into the dip of her lower back, onto her hips, and down the flank of her legs.

Whack. The stinging impact of his hand took her breath. She gasped with the bloom of heat. A surge of possessiveness, this time the claim she had for him, washed over her. Another slap. And another, creating a pattern of delicious friction against her flesh. She sucked in a breath as his touch gentled and slid over her buttocks, then lower, between her legs and into the wet heat of her sex.

Her head dropped between her shoulders. Melting warmth rushed through her.

"Only mine." He slid two fingers into her channel, gathered her cream, then brought his fingers to his mouth and sucked them.

"Please," she begged.

Luca moved in front of her and parted the fly of his jeans. She opened her mouth, desperate for a taste. His cock thrust forward.

"Lick," he said.

She touched her tongue to the pearl essence seeping from the slit. She closed her eyes, savoring the salty-sweet flavor. Leaning forward, she tried to take more of his length into her mouth.

Luca fisted his hand in her hair, stilling her movement. "Lick," he said again.

Swirling her tongue around the ridge, she tasted, licked, and kissed. More of his pre-cum coated her lips. She wanted more, to drive him as crazy as the way he made her mad with lust. But he stepped back, depriving her of power over him.

Her gaze focused on his hand as he lifted the flogger and rolled the handle in his palm.

The first tingling brush of the falls landed on her buttocks. The warmth of the spankings numbed the intensity. With a figure eight movement, the strikes crisscrossed her thighs. She relaxed into the sting. Her muscles liquefied. The drone of the snapping tails became music in the room.

Luca's harsh breaths matched her own. She could anticipate the imminent pain, the ripples of pleasure, and the teasing strain of denied release. He was relentless, inflicting his discipline with precision and power.

She moaned as the strikes landed on her shoulder blades, above the arm binding. Sweat trickled along her temple. With each thrashing hit, she gasped. She licked her dry lips. Another strike. Her body floated on a high of endorphins. A kaleidoscope of surreal colors exploded behind her closed eyes.

"Mine to discipline, mine to fuck."

His voice slipped through the haze, surrounding her in a dark, protective cloak. His firm fingers gripped her hips. And then he was there, his hot, hard cock filling her, driving deep, disintegrating any resistance lingering within her.

"Mine to love," he whispered.

Yes, she was his.

She cried out, crashing into a sea of sensations, each one a rolling wave, drowning her in the dark waters of submission. Uncontrollable tremors racked her. Cream slicked her pussy as he continued to pound into her, a man driven to dominate her.

His roar of release rent the air. Buried to the hilt, he erupted. Powerless to resist, she tumbled with him, another orgasm stealing her breath and shattering her walls. She quivered around his thick cock, filling and stretching her.

Luca loosened the ties and freed the harness. The binding slipped from her arms. She groaned as the blood rushed into her shoulders, pinpricks of pain shooting through her muscles and joints. The straps fell away, then she was in his arms.

Ignoring the pain, she wound her arms around his shoulders. Opening her mouth over his neck, she tasted his skin. She kissed, and she sucked, marking him as hers.

He settled her on the bed. "Cream, for your back?"

"Poppy keeps it in the bathroom."

Luca stepped from the room.

She pulled her knees to her chest and rounded her back. When he returned, he sat on the edge of the bed, opened the jar, and kissed her shoulder.

"When I come home from Protocol, sometimes, Poppy has to treat my skin." She felt the need to explain.

"Poppy will no longer need to worry. You're my responsibility now. Your aftercare is my responsibility."

She glanced over her shoulder.

He touched her cheek. "I told you before. I protect what is mine."

Mine to love.

"And I defend what's mine." She turned and took his hands in hers. "I know you want the truth about your family, and when you find it, you'll want revenge." She met his gaze with determination of her own. "I want retribution for you."

"And what if my family is tied to yours? Mia, the Thomas name is not unknown to my family. Our families were not allies, but enemies."

"My fight is not with you, and I'm not responsible for the decisions my parents made."

"Which is why this isn't your fight."

"No, it's yours…and so am I. This becomes our fight." She took a deep breath. "You have choices. I know your world is dangerous. I trust you to protect what is yours. So, if you want me, then take all of me."

He smiled. "I've already collared you." His fingers traced her collarbone, curving into the dip and ghosting over her flesh where he'd left bruises along her neck. "Would you have me take your soul? If you become like me, your heart grows black."

She kissed his lion's head ring. "Whatever it takes to destroy those who tried to destroy you."

***

After their afternoon in bed, decisions had been made. He may have lost his claim to the Bruno dynasty, but he would create a new empire with Mia at his side. He had no delusions of his need for her. That need had nothing to do with her wealth.

He loved her.

Luca tugged on his jeans. "Are you hungry?"

"Starving." She flipped through her closet, selecting a top with a high collar and billowy long sleeves.

"No clothes."

She laughed. "This isn't High Protocol."

He crossed to her and pulled her into his arms. "*Bellissima.*" He cupped her breast as he nuzzled her neck. Sex and innocence. Her scent was madness. His cock hardened, and his hands clenched. "Don't deny me the pleasure of seeing my marks on your body."

She whimpered, and her arms dropped to her side. The blouse fluttered to the floor.

"This." He pulled a sheer dress from the closet. "When you're ready, come to the patio. We will let Carlo and Hudson know of our plans."

"It's important that they both know that decisions come from you."

Luca nodded, then walked out of the bedroom. He needed to speak to Carlo. His leg ached as he took the stairs, but Mia's doctor had served him well. A man who could be trusted in the future should the need arise. He had no doubt there would be a need. More blood would be shed until he found those responsible for the attempt on his life.

And he would give Mia the truth on her parents. Even if it meant making a new enemy of the Bruno family.

He stopped in the kitchen. Poppy pulled pastries from the oven.

"You have a full house now." Luca crossed to the wine rack. He selected a cabernet. His sweet submissive had ordered in an extensive selection from the Bruno vineyards. "You'll need help here in the house."

"Bah." She wiped her hands on a tea towel. "I like to stay busy."

"Mia is coming down to the patio. Would you like to join us for a drink?"

She smiled. "Yes, thank you. I'll be out in a minute." She gathered the pastries onto a plate. "I'm glad you're here for her. She needs a good man in her life. I think you're good for her, and I want her to be happy."

"I intend to spend my life giving her what she needs."

Luca grabbed three glasses and the bottle of wine.

Outside, Carlo sat with Hudson. Luca considered the deadly bodyguard. He would protect Mia, but would he be willing to swear his allegiance to a Mafioso? To remain here, he would need to declare his loyalty to Mia, and she had already declared her loyalty… to him.

He sat at the table with them.

Hudson leaned back in his chair. "We need to talk about what happens now."

"We wait for Mia. No *family* decisions are made without her."

Carlo lifted a brow.

Luca met Hudson's stare. "I know you care for her. You have protected her. I'd like you to continue to protect her. But not from me. What I do with her and *to her* is none of your concern. I promise you I'm not interested in overtaking the Thomas wealth."

Hudson curled his hands into fists. "No, you're just going to hurt her."

Carlo chuckled and lit a cigarette. "Let it go," he said to Hudson. "I've seen it." He inhaled. "He's a kinky motherfucker, and she's into it."

Mia stepped from the house. Her hair hung in loose curls around her shoulders. A light breeze molded the sheer dress to her lithe body. A bra and panties covered her, but her neck and arms revealed the intensity of their afternoon in the dungeon.

Luca stood. He collared her neck with his fingers, bringing his face to hers. "*Bellissima.*" He kissed her.

"Christ," Hudson said, seeing the bruises and redness of her back and thighs. "I need a drink." His chair scraped the tile as he stood.

"Then pour the wine," Luca said to Hudson. "It's a good year." He pulled a chair next to his for Mia. Once she sat, he lowered into the seat next to her.

Poppy approached with pastries and two more wine glasses. After one glance at Mia, she turned her gaze to Luca. "See, I'm right. You're exactly who she needs."

I am. She waited for the man who would own her, to lock her away in the safety of a Dom's dungeon. She waited for me. But our fates intertwined long ago. She's destined to be a part of my dark and dangerous Mafia world. One day soon, she'll know the sweet taste of revenge.

** This was Luca's and Tinker's love story. However, there are some unanswered plot points about the Bruno Mafia Family to be revealed in the new, Bruno Family Dark Mafia Series. Look for Marco Bruno's story in 2023!

Dear Reader,

I hope you enjoyed Perfectly Played - Initiation into Submission: High Protocol Book Six

Damaged – Initiation into Submission: High Protocol Book One

Did you miss Alex and Evelyn's story? Download your copy or read for free on Kindle Unlimited!

The crack of his whip...her initiation into submission.

Evelyn Larsen is numb. She's lost her job, her lover…and herself. She doesn't want love or passion, but she does want to feel again. She wants the pain of BDSM…even if it means she'll have to endure the pleasure.

Businessman and Dom, Alex Ferraro isn't interested in anything more than scenes in his dungeon. But the haunting look in Evelyn's eyes draws him in. Under his control, he could set her free. But once his, will he be able to let her go?

Brutally Honest - Initiation into Submission: High Protocol Book Two

Misty's T-shirt says it all. Don't yuck someone's yum. Her yum? Judge and Kinbaku master Avery Lyons and his ropes.

The bonds of his rope…her initiation into submission.

Misty Kemp isn't submissive. She's fun, feisty, and isn't afraid to ask for what she wants. When asked to attend the City Gala, she trades her steel-toe work boots for garters and high heels…and meets the hot, newly elected Judge Avery Lyons.

Avery stepped away from the BDSM scene, giving up his rope when he put on the judge's robe. Since then, he's been hiding behind the bench, afraid of what discovery would do to his family and career. But Misty has his fingers itching to play. Getting involved is risky. She's not the kind of girl to be tied up, not even at the hands of a Kinbaku master.

She was supposed to be a one-night stand…or two. But he wants more and is willing to be brutally honest to prove it.

Forbidden - Initiation into Submission: High Protocol Book Three
Get to know the elusive and naughty Dom of High Protocol – Ronan.

Saying his name…her initiation into submission.

Two things change a person—love and grief. Domestic violence councilor, Claire Orion shares both with her best friend Gavin. He's seen her at her darkest moments, held her through the storms of her life. She wants more, but he's kept a secret from her. In his world, he's called Ronan. He wants to hurt her, to chase the pain with pleasure.

High Protocol Manager, Gavin Sears has always loved sweet and innocent Claire. She is his island, a special place untouched by the BDSM world he lives in. He wants one touch, one taste, one time. But once will never be enough. When he gives in to forbidden desires, will she see her submission as beautiful…or abusive?

Beautiful Liar – Initiation into Submission: High Protocol Book Four

Get to know Lyric with her scars and tattoos and the sexy Dr. Brooks Leighton. He wields a whip and has a seductive bedside manner.

The trust he earns…her initiation into submission.

Lyric Jones is a beautiful masochist. The scars across her body tell a dark and twisted tale. She aches for the pain of BDSM, but she lies to keep from being pulled back into the dangerous world she craves. She lies to hide her secrets. And she'll lie to protect the man who would make her his.

Dr. Brooks Leighton is immediately drawn to the submissive woman in his office. He's the match to her dark and tormented needs. If only she'll trust him with the secrets camouflaged in the butterflies and musical notes tattooed across her body. She is the music of his soul, but he'll drown in the silence of losing her unless he can show her she's safe in his arms.

Dangerously Bound - Initiation into Submission: High Protocol Book Five

Gabriella Ricci has a new bad boy boyfriend. Vance is determined to show her that she belongs on the back of his motorcycle…and chained to his bed.

The protection he gives her…her initiation into submission.

Gabriella Ricci is formidable in the office, but her personal life is a mess. Attractive men intimidate her and those she's trusted most have lied and betrayed her. When she meets a hot, tattooed bad boy, she takes a chance and climbs onto the back of his motorcycle. With Vance, she discovers a wild, reckless need for the BDSM pleasure promised in his bed.

Conformity was never a concern for Vance, until his high-risk lifestyle collided with responsibility.

Now he's on the right side of the law. Although he's unapologetic in his pursuit of pleasure, his past carries a cost he's still paying. He'll never be good enough.

Insecurity runs deep within her, and Vance struggles with forgiveness. Are they opposites, destined to constantly push against each other? Or maybe they're less screwed up together.

Dangerously Bound begins the Heller Raiders MC romance series. Bad boy bikers, dangerous drama, and lots of steamy sex. These are gritty stories including violence, drug use and graphic language. Get ready for a wild ride.

About the Author

KyAnn Waters is a multi-published, award-winning author of romance. She lives in Utah with her husband. Her two boys are grown and out in the world making mischief of their own. Never believing she was a pet lover, she still has made a home for a menagerie of animals. She enjoys sporting events on the television, thrillers on the big screen, and hot scenes between the pages of her books.

KyAnn loves to hear from readers. kyannwaters@hotmail.com

Visit her website www.KyAnnWaters.com

Books By KyAnn Waters

*After Dark
*All Lycan's Eve
*Beautiful Liar
*Beautiful Storm
*Bent For His Will
*Betrayed Vows
*Born Into Fire
*Borrowing the Bride
*Brutally Honest
*Cinderella Undercover
*Damaged
*Dangerously Bound
*Dark Man: Blood Slaves Book 3
*Delicious Darkness
*Double Bang!
*Eternal Rapture
*Executive Positions
*Forbidden
*Going Down Hard
*Hard Ride Home
*Her Cowboy's Command
*Hot Blooded
*Ice Man: Blood Slaves Book 1
*Impulsive Pleasures
*Iron Man: Blood Slaves Book 2
*Johnny Loves Krissy
*Just Kiss Me
*Mercy of the Dragon

*Miranda's Rights
*Perfectly Played
*Private Lessons
*Roped and Branded
*Rough Justice
*Striker
*Syre
*Taking Command
*The Cougar Meets Her Master
*The Highlander's Improper Wife
*The Highlander's Unexpected Bride
*The Naughty List
*The Rented Bride
*Tie Me Up, Tie Me Down
*To Bed a Montana Man
*To Serve and Protect
*To Wed a Wanton Woman
*Twisted Sex and Happenstance
*Up Close and Personal
*Wanderlust
*Weekend Boyfriend
*With or Without You

Printed in Great Britain
by Amazon